Combat General

By WILLIAM CHAMBERLAIN

Cover drawing by Albert Orbaan

SCHOLASTIC BOOK SERVICES

Published by Scholastic Book Services, a division
of Scholastic Magazines, Inc., New York, N. Y.

About the Author

William Chamberlain was born in the Salmon River country of central Idaho. After graduating from West Point he served through the grades in the artillery, infantry and Air Corps, being retired with the rank of brigadier general in 1946. In addition to COMBAT GENERAL, he is the author of COMBAT STORIES, and sixty other military stories, all of which appeared in the *Saturday Evening Post*.

Single copy price 45¢.
Quantity prices available on request.

Copyright © 1963 by William Chamberlain. This Scholastic Book Services edition is published by arrangement with The John Day Company, Inc.

1st printing....................................March 1965

Printed in the U.S.A.

COMBAT GENERAL

Until he arrived in Belgium to join the Hammerhead Division days before an impending German tank breakthrough, Brigadier General Miles Boone had been forced to sit out World War II at a desk in Washington. In fact, he had grown almost accustomed to being referred to as a "Pentagon general." But he never liked the term, and he knew that once he came under fire he would prove his worth as a commander.

When the assault came, Boone had the best assistant a combat general could ask — Sergeant Lute Heard, his driver and orderly, who had worn the Army's cloth for more years than either of them liked to admit. Before it was all over, both had seen more fighting than they wanted to see again.

In this story of front line action between American and German armored units, a detailed knowledge of men at war and their machines is the keynote — a sure knowledge acquired personally by the author in several combat theaters around the world.

One

THEY LEFT THE MEUSE at Dinant and turned northeast. Headquarters of the Hammerhead Division, Armored, was at a village named Couteaux some fifteen miles south of Liège — so they'd been told in Paris. The mid-December day was overcast and getting colder as the afternoon wore on. This highway had been ravaged by the battering transport of war, and now and then they passed engineer working parties as the command car lurched over the imperfectly filled holes in the roadbed.

Brigadier General Miles Boone sat alone on the hard leather of the back seat in the high-slung, ungainly vehicle; his roll and his musette bag were piled at his feet. He was a slender, medium-tall officer of thirty-nine. His gray eyes were thoughtful behind sharply carved features and he had the hands and legs of a cavalryman. Faintly hollowed cheeks gave his face a look of brooding watchfulness; he smiled seldom but when he did the expression had a warmth which surprised those who did not know him well.

The brigadier general's stars he wore on shoulder and collar were not yet a month old and he was a little self-conscious of their newness. Back at Supreme Headquarters Allied Expeditionary Forces (SHAEF), where he'd gotten his orders to the Hammerhead Division, he'd been aware of the covert looks and the vague hostility of people — even old friends — whom he'd run into. He didn't have to be told what they were thinking. It had been plain enough.

"Pentagon general, huh? Sat on his duff behind a desk for four years — now he comes over here to get a little glory rubbed off on him after most of the shooting is over and the war is practically a shoo-in the rest of the way."

And they'd be right — as far as they went, Miles Boone was thinking dourly now as the command car jolted over the road which alternately climbed and dipped as it made its way across rolling country occasionally patched with woods. He had been at a desk in the War Department in Washington for better than four years, but his long stay there had been no wish of his. Ever since Pearl Harbor he'd been eating his heart out to get away from the staff and to a command overseas. He'd tried. Each time until now he'd gotten a flat "no" for an answer. He couldn't be spared. His time would come later on, they'd said.

Sergeant Luther Heard, riding in the front seat beside the driver, turned his head so that the fading afternoon light showed on his red, hatchet-sharp face. Lute Heard had worn the Army's cloth for twenty-five years and the vicissitudes of his service showed in the gullies which etched eyes and mouth.

"I figure maybe an hour more," he said.

"About," Miles agreed absently.

"Not that I'm in any giddyap of a rush," Heard grunted. "I don't figure that they'll have no red carpet out and the band drew up waitin' to greet us."

A brief, tight smile showed on Boone's dark face for a moment. "I'd say the odds were against it, Lute," he said. "I'll try and bear up under the disappointment."

Heard grunted again and turned back to watching the road ahead. He and Miles Boone had known each other for a long time; they had been serving together in the Army's only armored brigade in the summer of 1940 when Miles had first been ordered to the general staff in Washington. Later Lute had fought in North Africa with the First Armored Division; in Italy he'd been wounded in the breakout from Anzio and had been shipped back to a hospital in the States. He'd been on training duty at a camp in Kentucky ten days ago when the Pentagon had finally made good on its promise and had released Boone for an assignment overseas.

Lute had learned of Boone's orders through the grapevine. He'd wasted no time bootlegging a ride on a plane to Washington and had camped on Boone's doorstep until the latter had consented to bring him to the European Theater of Operations (ETO) as his orderly. Lute Heard was an old soldier who knew all the ropes and he had a way of getting what he wanted. This time his argument had been potent.

"For Pete's sake, Miles," he'd said — when they were alone Lute was apt to be careless with military formality — "I taught you your horse cavalry when you were a second John green out of West Point, didn't I? Taught you good, too. How do you figure you can get along without me now?"

"What I ought to do is ship you back to Fort Knox as an AWOL, you old fraud," Miles had said. "Haven't you got a bellyful of being shot at by now?"

Lute had squinted slyly. "Be with you, won't I? Whoever heard of a general gettin' shot at?"

Miles had given in. "I have a feeling I'm going to regret this," he'd said. "All right, I'll have your orders cut."

"Don't need to bother. I already seen to it."

Boone had been secretly pleased, however. At least he'd have one friend when he hit the European Theater of Operations, he reflected; he wasn't too sure that he'd have any more. During his years in the War Department he'd had to tramp on too many toes; he'd had to chop and let the chips fall where they would and if, in the chopping, people had gotten hurt, it was just too bad. It was that streak of hardness in him that made him invaluable in the job he'd held down in the Pentagon rat race where everyone, big and small, had his own ax to grind whether or not the grinding fitted in with the picture of a war being fought all over the world.

But what had gone before wasn't going to roll out any red carpets for him now, Boone thought wryly. A major general at SHAEF had made that pretty clear yesterday when he'd told Miles of his assignment. The two had sat in a big, high-ceilinged office, and outside, clerks — hundreds of them, it had seemed to Boone — had moved without hurry about their duties. The war had seemed almost as far away there as it had seemed in the Pentagon.

"We're sending you up to the Hammerhead Armored, Boone," the two-star general named Hankins had said, giving Miles an oblique look. "The assignment was direct from Washington. Major General Clark Blocker commands the Hammerhead. You know him?"

"I know him," Boone had said.

Again Hankins had given him that sidelong look. "Benny Martell, who had Combat Command B of the division, was killed on the Roer last month. You're his replacement."

"All right," Boone said.

Hankins had watched him with a covert curiosity as he'd played with a letter opener. "Blocker has been informed of your assignment. We expected that he'd raise merry Cain about it," Hankins had gone on bluntly. "We expected that we'd have to cram it down his throat — say that it had been suggested by the Pentagon. Blocker thought a lot of Benny Martell. Considered him a topflight officer. We didn't think he'd be too happy . . ." He had stopped, letting the sentence hang.

"With a general who's spent the war behind a desk," Boone had said roughly. "Let's not be coy about it, General."

"You said it, not I," Hankins had answered blandly. "Anyway, Blocker didn't put up any beef about your assignment. I suppose your being a friend of his explains it."

"I'm no friend of his," Miles Boone had said and enjoyed the startled look that had come to Hankins' face. "To the best of my knowledge Blocker hates my guts."

Hankins had been momentarily shaken out of his smug complacency. "Well," he'd said feebly, "that will be jolly! Why didn't Blocker protest the assignment if that's the way he feels? It doesn't make sense!"

Miles Boone had smiled a faintly wintry smile. "I imagine General Clark Blocker has his own reasons," he had said.

"Well, that's it," Hankins had answered in the tone of a man washing his hands of the whole affair. "I can't say that I envy you, Boone. Blocker is a hard man to serve under, even when he likes you. He is liable to be unqualified poison if he doesn't like you."

Boone had been standing, too. Outside, clerks dawdled at desks and files. A knot of staff officers went by, laughing as they came from a coffee break. Poison or not, he thought, it's better than this. I ought to know — I've had four years of it. He took the hand which Hankins belatedly held out to him.

"I'll try to bear up under it," he'd said.

"There's another who's not going to be happy to see you take over Combat Command B," Hankins murmured. "Colonel Nash, commanding the armored regiment, has been in acting command of CCB since Benny got killed. He's been expecting that the War Department would pin a star on him and give him the combat command. I imagine he's going to be put out when you show up."

"I didn't come over here to run in a popularity contest," Boone had said shortly. "It's been nice seeing you, General. If you'll give me a car I'll be on my way."

Now the command car bumped over the cobbles as they passed through a small village. A town that hadn't been fought through, Boone thought idly; the houses bore no scars of war. People looked from the windows, some friendly, some sullen. Miles wondered at the latter. This was Belgium and these people should have been glad to see the Germans go and the Americans come. Well, it was no business of his. In the front seat the driver, a headquarters corporal, was again trying hard to impress Lute Heard with the fact that he had been over here since Normandy.

"Yeah," he was saying with an offhanded casualness — he'd noted the Stateside patch Lute wore — "it's been real rugged, I can tell you. Now you take them buzz bombs. There's a lot of nights when you hardly don't get no sleep at all."

"No!" Lute said, his voice shocked. No one except an old cavalryman would have noticed the faint bulge in Lute's cheek where he had stowed his quid of tobacco. "Buster, my heart shore bleeds for you pore guys. No sleep!"

"Well, not hardly any. You hear them bombs come chuffin' along. Then, when the engine cuts out, you know that you got real trouble. Four — five seconds later — *ker-wham!*"

"My," Lute said. "They ought to give you a Purple Heart. Or anyhow a Good Conduct medal."

The day was beginning to gray. They passed a company of Negro engineers loading road-mending tools into trucks. Boone caught a glimpse of grinning white teeth in black faces as they went by; one soldier drew himself to an exaggerated attention and turned out a British-type salute. Miles could hear the laughter of the others as it faded behind him. He knew it for what it was. Not a gesture of insolence or disrespect; it had simply been a little clowning which had broken the monotony of war for a moment.

"I figure us guys back in the States didn't really know how lucky we was," Luther Heard was saying blandly. "I figure we had it real good. I got to take my hat off to you guys that has been fightin' over here all that time."

"Yeah, it's been pretty tough, I tell you," the corporal agreed complacently. "What with the buzz bombs . . ."

"Now, that's one thing that I reely got to hand Anzio," Lute said wickedly. "We didn't have no buzz bombs."

There was a long silence while the command car climbed to the top of a rolling hill and began to drop into the valley on the other side. A half dozen miles away, dim in the waning afternoon, were the buildings of a town. Couteaux, Miles guessed. The driver was looking cautiously at Lute Heard out of the corners of his eyes now. He pulled his attention back to his driving.

"Were you at Anzio?" he asked finally in the tone of a man who knew he wasn't going to like the answer that he got. "I mean the beachhead at Anzio?"

"Yup."

"Uh, I guess it was quite a fight?"

Lute spat. "Why, no, sonny," he said casually. "I don't guess you could call it that. We didn't have no buzz bombs, see? I can remember quite a few nights when I got some sleep."

Conversation languished in the front seat, the driver staring rigidly ahead at the road now. They crossed a small stream on a stone bridge and climbed another low hill. Off to the left the bivouac of an armored unit was tucked into some woods where a few leaves still clung to the almost naked branches of the trees. Another ten minutes would bring them to Couteaux and Clark Blocker, and Boone had no illusions as to the sort of reception that would be waiting for him. It would be rough. The feud between Blocker and himself went back a long way — more than twenty years. Clark had been a first classman at West Point then and Miles Boone had been a plebe. . . .

It had been afternoon then, too. Release from quarters had sounded and the two of them had met in the boxing room of the gymnasium, each accompanied by two seconds as custom required. Miles had issued the challenge, a plebe's right when he felt that he was being unfairly treated by an upperclassman. Ed Finley and Bill Low, his roommates, had been Boone's seconds. Ed was later captured on Corregidor; Bill died at Kasserine Pass.

Wally Kearns, a neutral first classman acting as referee, had offered a last chance to call off the grudge fight, as custom also required. His voice had sounded far away to Miles as the late sunlight came through the western windows of the boxing room. He'd kept his eyes on Clark Blocker's handsome, faintly arrogant face as he'd listened to Kearns's words.

"You're the challenger, mister," Kearns had been saying. "I will urge you to withdraw the challenge. There is no stigma attached to your doing so."

"I'll withdraw nothing," Miles had said through his teeth. "The challenge stands."

He'd heard the same urging from his two roommates ever since he'd issued the challenge five days before. "Try to get a little smart, Miles," they'd said. "Blocker is three inches taller than you — weighs forty pounds more. You're just going to take a beating. What will it buy you?"

"Nothing, maybe," he'd said doggedly. "I just can't take any more of his riding, that's all."

"All plebes get ridden. It's a part of the system!"

"Not the way he rides me," Miles had said. "Sure, all plebes get ridden and I expect to take my share. But Blocker is different. He puts something personal into it that I'm tired of taking. All right, so he doesn't like me. Well, I'm giving him a chance to show that with his fists!"

It hadn't lasted long. The gloves, scarred from a thousand bouts in plebe boxing class, were pulled on. The two men moved to the center of the ring; the two pairs of seconds faced each other from opposite sides of the ropes. Kearns lifted a hand.

"No rounds," he said. "The fight will go on until one of the parties either cannot continue or says that he has had enough. Ready, gentlemen. Time!"

Mark Blocker stabbed twice with his left hand, jolting blows that rocked Boone's head back and put the salty taste of blood onto his lips. He couldn't hope to box with the heavier, taller man, Miles knew. Blocker could stand off and cut him into pieces with that wicked left hand. His only hope was to charge wildly in, hoping to get home a lucky blow.

He ducked and charged, swinging both hands, and saw blood spurt darkly from Clark Blocker's nose as his right hand landed. A solid blow but it hadn't been enough. Blocker backed away as he caught the next blow; his eyes narrowed and there was no expression in them as he weaved a little. Then a left hook caught Miles on the point of the chin, jarring him to his heels as everything went black.

He came to seconds later, that salty taste of

blood again in his mouth as his seconds supported him and massaged the back of his neck. Clark Blocker and his seconds stood a few feet away, looking at him noncommittally as they talked in low voices. After a moment Clark Blocker came forward.

"Satisfied, mister?" he asked.

"No," Miles had said through split lips. "I'm not satisfied! I'll fight you again, Blocker!"

A faint puzzlement came into Clark Blocker's face. "Why, mister?" he asked. "You know you can't beat me."

"I'll keep coming at you just the same," Miles said. "One of these days I will beat you, Blocker!"

They had fought twice more that spring and each time the result had been the same. Then Clark Blocker had graduated and gone into the field artillery and, three years later, Miles had been commissioned in the cavalry and somehow their paths had not crossed again until that afternoon in the Pentagon, more than two years ago now. Miles had worn the silver leaves of a temporary lieutenant colonel and he'd been holding down a desk in Operations while he wished that he were somewhere else.

He'd been smarting over the latest "no" to his request for troop duty on that afternoon when Clark Blocker had come into his office, wearing a full colonel's eagles and the triangular patch of an armored division on his shoulder. He'd looked at Boone behind the desk, then let his gaze take in the pretty secretary at her own desk and other pretty girls in the office beyond.

"Well, if it's not old Miles Boone," he'd said, lowering his big frame carelessly into the chair beside the desk. "Pretty plush foxhole you've got here. Been here long?"

"Two years," Miles had said, feeling his face start to get red under the jeering amusement in the other's eyes. "I've been trying to get away . . ."

Blocker's laughter had interrupted him. "Yeah, yeah, I know," he'd said, looking sardonically along the beak of his nose. "That's what all of you desk soldiers say."

"I'm busy," Boone had snapped, his temper flaring. "If you've got something on your mind, Blocker, let's have it. If you haven't — good-bye. It was nice seeing you!"

Blocker's cynically amused smile had deepened. "Now, now," he had said, "you don't suppose I'd waste my time around this hutch if I didn't have something on my mind, do you? I'm chief of staff of the Hammerhead Armored Division, in case you didn't know. They told me that this was the shop where I could get our priority for overseas shipment moved up. That right?"

"That's right."

"Okay," Clark Blocker had said, waving a big hand with an arrogant assurance. "We're ready to go. Just see to it that we move by the end of the month."

It would do no good to tell Clark Blocker that priorities for divisional movements overseas had

been set up by the front office, Miles knew; it
would be useless to try and explain that his own
job was to implement the instructions he had received — issue the orders. He wasn't so sure that he
wanted to tell Clark Blocker that, anyway. Let
him think what he wanted to.

"No soap," he said flatly. "The priorities have
been set up and they stand. Now, if that's all . . ."

Clark Blocker got up, his face dark and angry
now. "Is that your final word on it, desk soldier?"

"It is."

Blocker's teeth had gleamed whitely beneath his
black mustache but his grin was without mirth.
"Pal," he said softly, "those lickings I gave you
when you were a plebe wouldn't have anything to
do with this, would they?"

"They would not."

"I think you're lying," Blocker said softly, and
Boone had felt the startled eyes of his secretary on
him. "Well, I won't forget this favor. I'll be seeing
you."

The command car was coming into the outskirts
of the small town now, its tires jouncing over the
cobbles. The street widened into a square and the
driver stopped the car before a two-storied house
bigger than the others. A sign indicated that within
was the headquarters of the Hammerhead Armored Division.

"This is it, sir," the driver said, still sulking
from the Anzio beating he'd taken from Lute
Heard.

Boone climbed down to the cobbles and Lute turned his marble-blue stare on the corporal beside him. "Don't just set there, sonny, with your tail glued to that seat," he said. "Give me a hand wrastlin' this gear — maybe it'll get you tired enough so's you sleep right through them buzz bombs tonight."

"Stack the stuff on the stoop and wait for me," Miles said. "I don't imagine I'll be long."

"Yes, sir," Lute grunted for the corporal's benefit. "If I was you I'd watch myself in the clinches in there, General."

The afternoon was far gone and the wind, which had come up as the day died, had a smell of snow in it now, Miles noted as he climbed to the stoop. He entered a front room which had been a parlor. Fat chairs and a sofa had been shoved into a corner but a fire burned in the fireplace. A colonel, sitting behind a table piled with papers in the center of the room, looked up as Boone came forward. His expression turned wary as he saw the too-new stars on Boone's collar and shoulder.

"General Boone?" he asked guardedly, getting to his feet but not offering his hand. "I'm Watson, chief of staff. I'll tell General Blocker that you're here."

He disappeared through a door to the left and Miles was alone in the room. He was aware that voices, which had been coming through a doorway opening to the rear, were suddenly lowered to cautious undertones. He caught words, though, that were more distinct than the rest.

"All heck will break wide open now."

Miles's mouth flattened out stubbornly. Well, let it, he thought, his gray eyes bleak. I didn't come here expecting hugs and kisses. A log cracked and fell in the fireplace, sending up a shower of red sparks.

The door to the left opened again and Colonel Watson stood holding it. "Come in, General," he said and Boone thought that he accented the rank a little too much.

He went by Watson and the chief of staff closed the door, shutting himself on the outside. Clark Blocker was sitting behind a desk, his closed fists resting on the polished wood. He looked massive in the fading light; his face was little changed as Boone remembered it. Darkly handsome and arrogant and ruthless. Boone halted and turned out his salute and waited.

Blocker chuckled mirthlessly. "So they kicked you out of the Pentagon, did they?" he asked. "Well, well."

Boone felt the palms of his hands grow damp but he controlled his voice. "Just say that I'm here, General," he said evenly. "I don't expect you to be pleased but you might as well know this — I expect to stay."

"You'll stay — until you make your first mistake," Clark Blocker said, his voice hard and impersonal. "I could have yelled my head off when SHAEF, in its high and mightiness, sent me a desk soldier with no combat experience to replace Benny Martell. I didn't. Would you like to know why, Boone?"

"What you do or don't do is your own business, sir," Miles said, keeping his voice indifferent. "I'm not asking you for any reasons."

"Well, you'd better," Blocker said, staring back at Boone over his closed fists. "Because it's your neck that is stuck out a foot. You make just one slip — just one — and I mean to chop it for you. Understand? I'd chop anyone else's, Boone, but it will be a particular pleasure to chop yours."

"I think that I *am* beginning to understand," Boone said, his temper starting to ride him now as he repeated more or less what Blocker had said to him in the Pentagon two years ago. "I wonder if that priority you didn't get back in Operations wouldn't have something to do with this."

Blocker didn't answer for a moment as he sat there looking back from beneath his heavy brows. There was more gray in the other's hair than there had been two years ago, Boone noted indifferently as he got his temper back under control. He knew Clark Blocker's reputation as a division commander. He was one of the best, just as the Hammerhead was one of the best of the armored divisions. Division and commander had been tempered under fire in North Africa, honed bright in Normandy, and whetted to their fine cutting edge in the drive across France.

And, despite the ruthless driving which had won him the nickname of "Bloody Blocker," Boone knew that the division liked its general. It walked with a high and clannish pride which reflected the tough-

ness of the man who led it. It wasn't going to roll
out any welcome mat for a desk soldier.

"That Pentagon business has nothing to do with
it, Boone," Clark Blocker said finally and, oddly
enough, Miles believed him then. "You boned up a
reputation for yourself of being tough — sitting
behind a desk. Well, I'll tell you right now that
you'd better be really tough because it's going to
take a tall man to stand in Benny Martell's boots!
And that's where you're standing. My own opinion
is that you won't fill them."

"I'll fill them," Boone said, a harshly rasping note
suddenly coming into his voice. "Keep your ax at
home, Blocker. I'll fill them!"

Blocker seemed not to hear; the expression on his
face had subtly changed so that for a moment
Miles glimpsed the pain that was hidden deep in
the other's eyes. "I loved Benny Martell like a
brother," Blocker was saying softly, half to himself
now. "We fought through two years of this war
together. Two years while you were eating regu-
larly and sleeping dry and warm at night — when
your foxhole was a desk."

"You think I wanted that?" Boone asked through
his teeth. "You're wrong if you say so!"

"Whether you wanted it or not is unimportant
now," Clark Blocker said indifferently. "The point
is, you were sitting cozy in Washington for the two
years that Benny was laying it on the line. Then,
when the law of averages ran out on Benny, *you*
come here to fill his shoes. Well, you'd better stand
tall."

"And you don't think I can do it."

"I don't think you can do it." The violence had gone out of Blocker's voice, leaving it flat and impersonal again. "Make no mistake about it, Boone. One slip and you're dead. I'll yank you out of Combat Command B fast. I'll send you back to the Pentagon to wear your star, if you've still got one by then. Is that clear?"

"It's clear," Boone said shortly.

"If you don't like the deal, now that you know what it is, you can ask to be reassigned. I'll approve your request. It will prove what I've always thought. You can't take it."

"General Blocker," Miles Boone said softly, "I've spent four years trying to get a field command. I've got one now and if you think you're big enough or tough enough to make me let go of it, just start swinging."

Lute Heard, with an old soldier's craft, had scavenged a jeep. He had loaded the gear in back and was waiting behind the wheel as Boone came down the steps from the stoop. Dusk was beginning to come down and clouds were piling up in the west. The general climbed to the seat beside Lute.

"Combat Command B's bivouacked at a farm 'bout a mile south of here," Heard grunted as he meshed the gears and let in the clutch. "How'd it go, Miles?"

"You were right," Boone said. "I didn't get any bouquets. That's okay. I didn't expect any."

The jeep bumped over the cobbles, leaving the square behind; it followed a narrow and winding street and then Lute turned it into a dirt road which led away and across the fields. A sign, with an arrow pointing, read: CP—CCB. Off to the left a dog bayed as dusk began to come down and the rising wind held the threat of snow.

"I was askin' around," Lute said, his tone a little too offhand. "I run into a sergeant I used to know in the First Armored in Africa. He says that this Benny Martell, that got himself knocked off on the Roer, was right well liked in CCB."

"So?" Miles asked, hanging on as the jeep bucked and lurched over the ruts in the dirt road.

"So CCB ain't goin' to like no new general that comes to take command," Lute grunted. "They wouldn't like him even if he was the Angel Gabriel himself. So it kind of looks like we might have our hands full."

"I expected that."

"Okay," Lute said resignedly. "Just so that you don't go wanderin' in there like no little lost lamb. I got a feeling that there's goin' to be plenty of gougin' and buttin' in the clinches before this thing is over."

They moved through a small fir copse and passed a field where tanks were parked too close together. Then they saw a stone house, light showing from its windows, a hundred yards ahead. Stone outbuildings flanked it. Their progress had been unslowed by the challenge of a sentry or any other security guard and Boone frowned, his mouth flattening into its stubborn line.

This was a rest sector, he knew, and the front was some forty miles to the east. Nevertheless, that was no excuse for not maintaining adequate security measures. Slack security meant slack discipline. Even more than that, there were probably German sympathizers about — he remembered those sullen faces he'd seen passing through that village earlier this afternoon after they'd left the Meuse. A handful of sugar in a gas tank could ruin an engine; a single match could set gasoline stores ablaze.

"No band here, either," Lute Heard said cheerfully, his good humor returning as he braked the jeep to a stop before the door of the farmhouse. "Could be they don't know we're comin' or could be they don't give a hoot."

"Bring the gear in," Boone said curtly.

He stepped down into churned mud, crossed a low stoop and shoved the door open unceremoniously. A wave of warm air, smelling strongly of herbs, struck his face as he crossed the threshold and stood just inside with the glare from a Coleman lantern lighting up his dark face. Three officers sat at a table in front of a kitchen fireplace playing cards. A major and two captains, he saw. The major, a burly and heavy-set man, sat with his back to the door. He spoke without turning his head.

"Come on in and shut the door, whoever you are," he said. "Where were you raised, in a barn?"

The two captains sat, their mouths a little open,

while they stared back at Miles. One had a long, lantern-jawed face; the other wore steel-rimmed, GI issue glasses which accentuated the roundness of his cheeks. Boone left the door open as he strode forward. The two captains were struggling to their feet now but the major was still hunched over his cards.

"I was raised in the back room of a saloon and I don't like fat majors who need a shave and who try to get tough with me," Boone said, and there was a soft wickedness in his voice which brought the pudgy officer up, his chair tipping backwards as he turned. "Right now I want to see whoever is in acting command of CCB and I want to see him fast!"

"Sir," the major said, stuttering a little and his eyes bugging as he took in Boone's stars, "Colonel N–Nash is in command. He went into Couteaux this afternoon. I . . . I don't expect him back until morning. I'm M–Major Summer, the executive officer. I'm sorry . . . I didn't . . . that is, we didn't think that the general was due to arrive until tomorrow . . ."

Boone brushed the words aside impatiently. "That's pretty obvious, Major," he said, his words cutting. "I rode in here just now without being challenged by anybody. An enemy saboteur could have done the same. I'd like to hear why this command does not seem to be observing even the most elementary of security procedures."

Major Summer was standing at a stiff attention now. "Sir," he said, his voice still shaky but resentment growing in his eyes, "Colonel Nash didn't consider it necessary to post any guards. This place is pretty far back and we've just come out of a hard fight on the Roer and Colonel Nash said that the combat command had some rest coming to it so that . . ."

Again Boone brushed the words aside impatiently. "Never mind what Colonel Nash said," he interrupted curtly. "Gasoline will burn just as quickly in a rear area as anywhere else if a collaborator puts a match to it. All right, I'm taking over. If you want to keep on being executive, Major, you shag out of here fast and see that a proper guard is set up. Get!"

"Yes, sir," Summer said in a scared voice.

He got a hand up in a shaky salute; then sidled around Boone and scooted for the door. Lute Heard, no expression on his weathered face, watched him go and then shut the door. It was beginning to drizzle outside. Now Miles laid his attention on the two captains standing on the far side of the table.

"You, Captain," he said to the lanky, lantern-jawed man, "what's your name?"

"Jeff'son, suh," the man said with a deep Southern accent. "Cap'n Leroy Jeff'son from Mobile, suh."

"What's your job?"

"S-3, suh."

"Go into Couteaux and find Colonel Nash. Bring him back with you. I want him here in a half hour!"

Captain Jefferson shifted his feet uneasily and glanced at the chubbier captain, who wore glasses.

"General, sir," he mumbled, "I don't know if I can find Colonel Nash. He didn't say exactly where he was goin', seh, you see."

"I see all right," Boone said grimly. "You bring him back with you if you have to take a truckload of men and comb the town. You, with the glasses, what's your name?"

"Captain Potts, sir," the chubby officer said. He was regarding the general with a placid interest now that he had recovered from his first surprise. He didn't volunteer the rest of his name or his home town. He just added, "S-2, sir."

Boone liked that as he glanced at the watch on his wrist; it said 1810. "All right, Captain," he said. "I want to see all unit commanders here at 2000. Take that word to each of them personally. Got it?"

"Yes, sir."

Potts went, moving neither fast nor slow as he closed the door behind him. Lute Heard came up to the table, the bright glare of the Coleman lantern highlighting the sharp planes of his face. He glanced at the cards scattered on the blanket which covered the table. A poker hand had been faced there.

"Aces an' eights," Lute murmured. "The dead man's hand — I hope it ain't no omen, Miles. Well, I got to say you give them birds the shock treatment, all right."

"I was a dirty word to them before I ever got here," Miles said indifferently. "I may as well live up to the part. There's a smell around here that I don't like, Lute. Martell may have been a topflight combat commander himself but I've got my doubts about Nash. Things aren't right. No security . . . tanks jammed together as though they were on a Washington parking lot . . . a fat major, needing a shave, running the show."

"You know Nash before, Miles?"

"Not well. I know that he comes from an old and distinguished Army family but it looks like the line has gone to seed. He graduated a class ahead of me at the Point. Add that to the fact that he expected to get a star and keep command of CCB and it's not likely to spell out anything except trouble ahead."

"I wouldn't bet against it," Lute said piously. "Especially after that Dixie captain drags him back here from town. Well, I better see to gettin' that jeep back to division, I reckon. No use for our popularity takin' any worse beating than it has to. See you later."

He went out and Miles Boone stood for a moment, scowling at the fire, as the flare of temper died in him leaving, as it always did, a feeling of being spent and a little older. Closed doors were at either end of this long kitchen, he noted absently; as they'd driven up in the dusk he had observed that the building was big and rambling. The country seat of some well-to-do Belgian, he supposed. Deeper in the house a door banged as though it had been blown shut by a sudden draft coming through open windows.

He tried to shake off his glum thoughts as he turned to a refectory table at the side of the room, its top littered with maps and papers. He shouldn't have sent that S-2 off so suddenly, he decided. He needed someone who could fill him in a little on the combat command. It had been resting and re-fitting here near Couteaux for about ten days, he knew; what state of battle readiness it possessed was something that he had to find out.

Today was December 14, and back at SHAEF yesterday they'd told him that no major action, other than continuing operations against the Roer dams, was contemplated before the first of the year. Boone had stood in front of the big Operations map while a bored lieutenant colonel from Intelligence briefed him. The map symbols showed that only six divisions held the Ardennes front from a point forty miles east of Couteaux, where the Hammerhead Armored lay, along the line of the Our River running south in a westerly bulge, to Echternach. Seventy-five miles of line.

"What about down here?" Boone had asked, putting a finger on that westerly bulge. "Pretty thinly held, isn't it, Colonel? The Germans might consider it inviting enough to try an offensive of their own, I should think."

The lieutenant colonel from Intelligence had given him a condescending look as he had slapped the pointer in his hand against the leg of his elegantly cut English slacks. His attitude said that he had no time to waste instructing Pentagon generals in such elementary matters of tactics and strategy.

"General," he'd said, "in the first place, the German is through — finished. He hasn't got the means to mount any sort of an offensive even if he was foolish enough to want to do so. In the second place, if he could mount an offensive, the Ardennes in December would be the last place he'd choose."

"He's chosen it three times before," Miles had said.

The Intelligence officer had shrugged, smoothing his neat mustache with a careful forefinger. "I assure you that all of the factors have been given the most careful consideration, General," he had said, not bothering to hide his impatience. "There has been no action in the Ardennes sector, except for a little routine artillery dueling, since early last fall. You don't need to be alarmed about it. It's the Ghost Front. Army has been sending its divisions down there for a rest after they've been pulled out of the line farther north. That's how quiet it is."

Despite the Intelligence lieutenant colonel's cocksureness, Boone had left the Operations room with a feeling of uneasiness that still persisted. That vague foreboding had been back of his decision to meet with his unit commanders tonight rather than let the matter go until tomorrow morning. An obscure hunch kept warning him that he'd better lose no time in getting his hands securely on the reins of Combat Command B.

A door opened and closed softly at one end of the room and Miles turned, the preoccupied scowl still on his face. He'd supposed that it was Summer or Potts returning, coming into the house by an-

other entrance. Now he saw that it was neither of
them. A woman was coming forward in the light
of the Coleman lantern and Boone's frown deepened. He had expected no woman here. Confound
it, he already had enough complications on his
hands!

She was slim and fairly tall, he saw. About thirty
and she had auburn hair which framed dark,
thoughtful eyes and a composed face. No peasant
woman. Not particularly pretty, Miles decided, but
there was breeding and poise in the way she moved
and pride in the level look she gave him.

"General Boone?" she asked in English.

Miles nodded, surprised and relieved that he
didn't have to struggle with his bad French. Her
voice was pleasantly modulated — a voice that
might have come from Pennsylvania or his own
home town in upper New York State. The hand
that she held out to him was cool and firm in its
brief clasp.

"I am Janet de Ceilly," she said. "I understood
from the other officers you were expected tomorrow. Since you have come tonight, instead, I
thought it only friendly to welcome you to my
home. I hope you will be comfortable here."

"You don't speak English — you speak American,"
Miles said, his voice more brusque than he'd meant
it to be. He'd had scant association with women
since his wife had died four years ago; he had
wanted none and long hours in the Pentagon had
given him ample excuse. "I mean — well, I guess
I didn't expect to find someone living here in Bel-

gium who spoke as though they came from Albany
or Troy . . . not that it isn't nice . . ."

He sounded like a stammering school kid, Miles
thought, angry with himself. He saw that Janet de
Ceilly was looking at him with a faint amusement
in her eyes. Her lips quirked faintly at the corners.

"I was born in Dobbs Ferry, N.Y., General," she
said. "I don't suppose you ever heard of it."

Two

IT WAS FUNNY, Miles Boone was thinking as he stood in the kitchen of this Belgian farmhouse looking back at Janet de Ceilly, how things out of a man's past could catch up with him. He supposed that he hadn't thought of Dobbs Ferry in twenty years.

"I spent Christmas Day there once," he heard himself saying. "It was a long time ago — when I was a cadet."

For a moment, in the long room with the smoking fireplace and the hissing Coleman lantern, that snowy day was very clear again. He'd been a second classman at the Point then and he'd taken Christmas leave just because he wanted to get away from the gray barracks on the Hudson. There was no sense in going upstate to the town where he had grown up; his parents were dead and there had been no one else in Hunter that he cared to see. So he'd picked Dobbs Ferry because the name had interested him a little and he'd crossed the Hudson and ridden south along the river on the New York Central Railroad and he had gotten off at Dobbs Ferry at midmorning on Christmas Day.

It had been an odd thing to do, he remembered.

He'd walked the snowy streets and looked at the big houses, set far back among the trees. He'd looked at the holly wreaths on the doors and he'd watched jingling sleighs go by, filled with laughing people his own age; everything was set and ordered here and fitted neatly into its frame. And he had suddenly known that this was not for him, so he had taken the afternoon train back to the gray fortress that waited for him up the river.

Miles Boone pulled himself away from his thoughts, aware that Janet was speaking again. "Dobbs Ferry is very beautiful at Christmas," she was saying. "It is nearly ten years since I have seen it — I always meant to take Paul back there with me for Christmas. Then the war came and it was too late."

"Paul?"

"My husband. He was killed at Louvain in 1940."

"I'm sorry," Miles said awkwardly. The words sounded inadequate but he couldn't think of anything better. "I hope you haven't been inconvenienced too much by us moving in here."

Janet stood in front of him, the light glinting on her hair, while she studied his face soberly for a moment. "General," she said at last, "I have lived with German occupation for more than four years. Do you think it possible that people — soldiers — of my own country could do anything I would not welcome?"

"It's good of you, Madame de Ceilly," Miles said, annoyed with himself that the stiffness still remained in his voice. "I don't imagine that we shall be here much longer. Meanwhile, we'll try to inconvenience you as little as possible."

"I have not been inconvenienced," Janet said. "Colonel Nash and the others have been very kind. Perhaps some time you will have tea with me and we can talk of Dobbs Ferry?"

There was no coquetry in the way she said it and Miles didn't know why it should annoy him that she mentioned Colonel Nelson Nash. It did, though, and the annoyance brought the brusqueness back into his voice as he answered.

"Thank you," he said. "I'm afraid that I shall be busy taking over the combat command."

"Of course," Janet said, half-turning toward the door. "May I ask you something? Forgive my ignorance, it is so long since I have been home to the States and things have changed."

"Ask, of course."

"I have heard the officers here speak of your coming, General. They said that you were a Pentagon general. That must be something quite special, is it not?"

Miles felt the color rising in his face and his eyes turned flinty as he looked down at Janet. He sought some hint of mockery in her expression. There was none. Her lips were parted a little as she looked back up at him and her gaze was candid and steady as it met his own.

"Yes, it's something quite special, madame," he said harshly. "It means that so far I have sat out this war behind a desk in the Pentagon. Now, if you will excuse me. . . ."

A company of one of the medium tank battalions was billeted in a cow barn and Butch Marcus, a tank commander, talked with Steve Reilly, his gunner. Butch had fixed his blankets up in a comfortable niche in a corner; a stub of candle, thrust into the neck of a wine bottle, stood on an empty ammo box and threw a flickering light over the stalls and the straw-littered floor. Chow hadn't been too bad tonight and now the two men settled down comfortably while they discussed the day's events.

"I hear Boone got in tonight," Butch said. "It raised quite a hoorrah. Seems like Nellie Nash an' the rest wasn't expectin' him until tomorrow. Summer is playin' poker with *Le*-roy and the fat boy when our new poobah blows in. Nellie is over in town an' nobody knows just where. I hear Boone takes it kind of hard."

"How kind of hard?" Reilly asked.

Reilly was twenty and freckled and he handled a tank gun with the dexterity of a man shooting skeet. "The best cockeyed gunner in the whole cockeyed army," Butch would say. And Butch ought to know because he was, by his own admission, the best cockeyed tank commander in the whole cockeyed army. The rest of CCB didn't argue with him about it. First, because it didn't pay to argue with Butch Marcus; second, because Butch was just about as good as he claimed to be.

"Boone went off like one of them V-2 rockets," Butch said with a faint satisfaction in his voice. "He sent *Le*-roy into town lookin' for Nellie. I heard *Le*-roy hollering for a detail to go along with him maybe a half an hour ago."

"Aw, well," Reilly said philosophically, "generals are like that — always mad. Maybe that's why they are generals. You get a good look at this one, Butch?"

"A little peek," Butch said. "I was by the corner of the farmhouse when this one comes up in a jeep. He's got a sergeant driver who I will bet has seen the inside of every guardhouse in the Army. That old rooster's been *a*-round."

"Nuts with about the sergeant," Reilly said. "What's with this new general, Butch?"

"Don't rush me — I'm comin' to that," Marcus grunted. "Well, he ain't too big and I didn't see him spittin' no carpet tacks but he's got a way of movin' and holdin' his head that reminds me of another guy I used to know. Don't look now, boy, but I'll bet this Boone can be suddener than a gunny bag full of rattlesnakes. I got a hunch that Nellie Nash had better watch his step or he's liable to find himself all spraddled out like a tromped-on frog."

"Well," Reilly said, yawning, "I can take my generals or let 'em alone. Who's running the poker game tonight?"

In the Ardennes, tangled mousetrap country broken by crisscrossing ravines and gloomy beneath hooded firs, nineteen German divisions — the muscle of three armies — moved into final position on the night of December 14, 1944. This

had been planned since late July — Hitler's desperate bid for a smashing victory in the west. It was
Operation Christrose, which would be known as the
Battle of the Bulge, and two mornings hence it
would explode through the fog like a hurricane.

Cloaked by night, infantry divisions moved
stealthily forward to their lines of departure. Low-
flying planes drowned the racket of diesel engines
as tanks — the Tigers and Panthers of the panzer
divisions — moved up to hiding places a scant six
miles behind the deceptively quiet front. Horse-
drawn and motorized artillery batteries crept cautiously to their assigned positions. Here, hidden by
the clammy darkness, a quarter of a million men
were on the move, weaving their complex patterns.

New railroads, hastily laid down and craftily
camouflaged, brought up huge stores of ammunition, fuel, food, engineer supplies to establish the
dumps that would feed the three armies. Farther
forward, corduroy roads, built with sly caution and
straw-covered to deaden the noise of wheels,
fanned out like fingers from the railheads. Ramps
were brought up to span the "dragon's teeth" of the
Siegfried Line so that the tanks might pass over.

Two days later was *Der Tag*.

At daybreak on the 16th Sepp Dietrich's Sixth
Panzer Army would strike in the north through the
Losheim Gap, sweep the Elsenborn Ridge, and drive
toward Antwerp. The Fifth Panzer Army, Baron
Hasso von Manteuffel in the saddle, would circle
the Schnee Eifel in the center, grab Saint Vith in its
stride, and then slam westward to the Meuse. On

the south, General Ernest Brandenberger's Seventh
Army would push through Echternach and pro-
tect the left flank of the deep penetration.

The crawling and stirring of a quarter million
men just beyond the Our on this second night
before the great offensive should have set some
sort of a wave in motion. It should have generated
an electric current which would have been strong
enough to send a warning tingle along the Ghost
Front held by only four American divisions, none
of them wholly combat-ready. Two of them were
so battle-ravaged that they had been sent here for a
rest; two of them were still green to battle. Some
taint of the cloud of hate building up to the east
should have been wafted westward to warn those
on whom that hate was to fall. It wasn't.

December 14th was a peaceful night at places
with such quaint names as Krinkelt and Losheimergraben and Krewinkel and Winterspelt. No one
worried that night in Saint Vith and Bastogne. Few
were concerned at Couteaux.

Colonel Nelson Nash was sitting in the parlor of a
prosperous farmhouse on the outskirts of Couteaux
when Captain Jefferson found him. Nash sat with his
field jacket off, his feet stretched toward the
warmth of a porcelain stove while he drank beer
and spoke excellent French with his host, a portly
burgher. Nash was tall and well built; handsome
with his wavy blond hair and sculptured features,
a fact of which he was well aware.

Four generations of Nashes had gone to West

Point and had made the Army their profession. Three of these generations had made general. It was only the stupidity of the War Department, so Nash believed angrily, that had kept the fourth generation of the clan from getting his star before now. An unbiased observer might have disagreed after he'd talked with Nelson Nash for a little while or had observed him with a clinical eye.

Such an observer might have concluded that the Nash stock had deteriorated a little from the hardy strain that had been present at Gettysburg and San Juan Hill and at Soissons and in the Argonne Forest. He might have noted a trace of weakness in Nash's mouth which was a little too wide-lipped; he might have thought there was a certain indecision in Nash's hazel stare. If he was a subordinate, though, he had better agree with Nash's estimate of the situation. The War Department was grossly stupid or it would have pinned stars on his shoulders before now.

Captain Leroy Jefferson from Alabama stood uncertainly in the parlor, turning his wool cap in his hands, while he met Nelson Nash's scowl. "Well," Nash snapped. "What is it, Jefferson? I told you I wasn't to be disturbed tonight!"

"Sir," Jefferson said unhappily, "General Boone's at the command post. He got in a half hour ago."

Nash's scowl deepened. "Division said he was coming tomorrow," he snapped pettishly. "As far as I'm concerned, he's still due tomorrow. If you've trotted out here just to give me the news, you've wasted your time."

The unhappiness deepened in Jefferson's long-jawed face. "Sir, General Boone said I was to tell you."

Color crawled up into Nash's face but his long body stayed sprawled lazily in the chair. "Oh, he did? Well, I'll see him tomorrow morning," he said indifferently. "I don't mean to ruin a pleasant evening just to rush back and scrape before some Pentagon general."

Real misery showed now in Jefferson's expression. Dogged if I ain't got my throat cut if I do or if I don't, he was thinking. I wish to Aunt Mary I was back home in Mobile right now. Dog if I don't. The portly burgher stared placidly from one to the other, not understanding.

"Colonel, sir," Jefferson tried to explain. "I guess you don't quite understand—"

"I said I'll be back tomorrow morning," Nash interrupted sharply. "You can tell him that. Then put him to bed — if he can't get there by himself."

Captain Jefferson's lantern jaw took on a stubborn set. "Colonel Nash," he said, "General Boone said that I was to bring you. He said I was to take a detail of men along with me if I had to. They're outside in the truck now."

Nash did move now. He sat bolt upright in his chair and his fair-skinned features showed a trace of shock. "He what?" he demanded as though he hadn't heard correctly.

"Told me to bring you, sir," Jefferson said doggedly. "He acts like a kind of a sudden guy, Colonel."

Nash stood up angrily. "I've a good notion to take this straight to Blocker," he said, but that faint uncertainty had come into his eyes and he knew that he wouldn't do it. He reached for his field jacket which was thrown over a chair. "Oh, all right! If I've got to baby him, I suppose I've got to. Come on!"

They rode back in the truck, not talking. The rain, promised by clouds which had piled up late in the afternoon, had begun to fall. It was a cold drizzle that would later turn to snow. The truck jolted over the ruts and wheeled through a fir copse as it neared the farm. A voice challenged hoarsely.

"Halt! Who's there?"

"Oh, for cripe's sake — playing soldier now, are we?" Nash said furiously under his breath. "I suppose that this is another of our Pentagon general's screwy ideas?"

"Yes, sir," Jefferson said cautiously. "He seemed right put out that he wasn't challenged when he drove in here, Colonel. He climbed all over Frank Summer about it."

"This is Colonel Nash," Nelson called crossly into the rain. "It's all right. You can let us by, soldier."

A shaky voice — that of a replacement by the uncertainty in it—came back through the night. "Sir, I'm kind of new at this an' the sergeant said I'd better do it by the book if I didn't want to get chewed out so I guess I better had. Dismount and advance one to be recognized . . . sir."

Swearing, Nash stepped down into the mud.

"What's your name, soldier," he began angrily and then gave it up. "I haven't got the password but I'm Colonel Nash. You've seen me around here. You recognize me, don't you?"

"Yes, sir, I seen you," the sentry said. "I guess it's all right. Pass, Colonel Nash, sir."

Gears clashed and the truck went on. A subdued murmur of men's voices was heard under the canvas hood behind. Nash sensed the speculation in their tones and it fed his anger. There'd be ways of putting this Boone in his place, he was thinking. Plenty of ways. The man had had no experience with an armored division; he knew nothing about how to run a combat command. Most important of all, he had never been in battle. Oh, there were plenty of ways. The truck stopped before the door of the farmhouse and Nash climbed down — he went up to the stoop, Jefferson behind him.

Miles Boone was standing in front of the fire as Nash and Jefferson came in, dripping from the rain; he stayed where he was, feet spraddled a little and his hands clasped behind his back as Nash came forward, taking his time, and stopped beside the blanket-covered table where the poker hands still lay. The colonel didn't salute but waited, hands propped on his hips, while Boone studied him for a moment from beneath knotted brows.

"You can go, Captain," Miles said then to Jefferson. "Be back here with the others at 2000."

Jefferson went hastily, closing the door carefully behind him. "You sent him with a detail of men for me, General," Nash burst out angrily when the two of them were alone. "I'd like to know why. Am I under arrest?"

"I sent for you because I wanted you," Boone said, his voice betraying nothing. "You are not under arrest." His voice sharpened. "Stand at attention, Colonel! We are not civilians meeting casually. Introduce yourself properly!"

That slow flush came back into Nash's face as he angrily jerked himself erect and turned out an exaggerated salute. "Colonel Nelson Nash, in acting command of CCB, reporting, sir!" he said. Boone returned the salute.

"Thank you, Colonel. I am General Boone. You knew that I was coming, I believe?"

Boone had chosen his words deliberately, a method in his choice. Of course Nash knew that he was Boone and that he was coming just as Nash knew that he was senior to Boone on the lists of the Regular Army. And Boone knew, too, that that rankled. Nevertheless, he had a job to do and, if it was to be done, there had to be no doubt as to who was running Combat Command B.

"I knew," Nash said sullenly.

"Very well," Miles said, dismissing the matter. "I didn't send for you, Nash, because I was annoyed not to find you here when I arrived. I sent for you because I found things here that a commanding officer should be attending to instead of absenting himself for personal reasons. I found that you'd taken no security measures, for one thing. Why?"

"This is a rest area," Nash said, controlling his

voice with an effort. "Combat Command B has just come out of a hard fight on the Roer. It deserves a little rest and not to be harassed by a lot of tom-fool training manual routine!"

"I see," Miles said, his voice toneless. "I passed a battalion of medium tanks parked like cars in a garage. A single bomb could knock half of them out. What about that?"

"Washington's pretty far away, General," Nash said, his edged words not quite reaching the verge of insolence. "We've had control of the air for a little while around here. I don't think we've anything to worry about from German bombs."

"They thought they didn't have anything to worry about from Japanese bombs at Pearl Harbor," Boone said. "From now on, Combat Command B exercises the same security measures that it would in the face of the enemy. We'll get on. You've been refitting here for ten days or so. What is your replacement status on tanks? Are all of them ready to roll?"

For the first time since he'd entered the room a little of the haughtiness seemed to leave Nash. He still stood at an aggressively stiff attention but Boone, watching without seeming to do so, had the impression that a little of the starch had gone out of the set of the other's shoulders.

"I don't have the exact figures at my fingertips, General," he said, his tone a little too casual. "I'll check on it — have the dope for you the first thing in the morning."

"You're commanding the armored regiment, in

addition to exercising acting command of CCB?"

"Yes, sir."

The mild note went out of Boone's voice; now it cracked as harshly as a whip. "Then why, by all that's holy, don't you know how many serviceable tanks you've got? Now? This minute? Why do you have to check up on it? Suppose we got a march order tonight? I'm waiting for your answer, Colonel!"

That slow red crawled up into Nash's face again. "Sir, I've been busy with other things . . ."

"Such as keeping up with your social life in Couteaux?" Miles snapped. "What's your personnel situation? How many replacements has the combat command received? Is it up to Table of Organization strength in men and officers? Do you know the answer to that?"

"No, sir."

Miles Boone moved away from the fire, coming to stand before Nash. He was shorter, slighter than Nash but the latter knew, with a sudden despair, that Boone was the better man of the two of them. It added fuel to his burning resentment.

"I know the fine record that your family has made back through the years, Nash," Miles was saying, the rasp gone out of his voice now. "A record to be proud of, yet everything that I've seen since I have been here shows that you are letting that record down. You're letting it down badly. Why?"

The flush had gone from Nash's face, now leaving it too pale; his full lips were almost bloodless as he pressed them too tightly together. Miles thought,

I've got to watch this man. He will come apart under pressure. Nash's voice was hoarse as he answered, staring over Boone's head.

"I don't think I've let anyone down, sir."

"You've let Combat Command B down," Miles snapped. "It was a fine fighting outfit when it came out of the Roer — the record proves that. Now, in less than three weeks, it's lost its edge. It's become slovenly. Answer me one question, Nash. If Benny Martell were still alive, commanding CCB, would there have been no guard set tonight? Would those tanks be parked out there in the field like a lot of commuter's cars? Would I have arrived to find the commanding officer off visiting in town and an unshaven major holding down the job here? What do you say? Would I?"

The answer was a long time in coming — Miles thought for a moment that it wasn't coming at all. "No, sir," Nash said at last, the words barely audible. The farmhouse kitchen wasn't warm but drops of sweat were trickling down his face now.

"All right," Boone said quietly as he moved back to the fire. "You asked me a little while ago if you were under arrest, Nash. You're not. You'll be my deputy in addition to continuing to command the armored regiment. I'll need your help in getting Combat Command B back into shape to fight again. When you report here at 2000 with the rest of the unit commanders, I'll expect you to have the answers to those questions I asked you earlier. Is that clear?"

"Yes, sir."

"One thing more," Boone added grimly. "I've already got one monkey riding my back. Don't give me another — you'll get hurt, if you do. I'll see you at 2000."

Nash's salute wasn't overelaborate this time. He'd gotten his facial expression back under control and he turned, without answering, and went through the kitchen door. He'd been gone only seconds when the door opened again and Lute Heard came in, his face wet and shining in the light. He kicked the door shut behind him and then came on to dump tin cans onto the blanket that covered the table, pushing the scattered cards out of the way.

"K-rations," he grunted. "If they got a headquarters mess around here, I ain't found it yet. Passed a guy goin' out that looked like he'd been bit by a dog. That Nash?"

"That was Nash," Miles said.

"Well, I said he wasn't goin' to love you," Lute said philosophically. "He's probably dreamin' up poison to put in your soup. Think you can stomach any of this garbage, Miles? I'm hungry enough to eat broiled skunk, myself."

The hand of Miles Boone's watch was on the dot of 2000 when Nelson Nash led his little procession out of the rain and into the glare of the Coleman lantern in the kitchen. They ranged themselves along the wall as Miles, who'd been sifting through the orders and reports and rosters that littered the refectory table, stood up and advanced to the center of the room. For a moment he stood there looking at them.

"I'm Boone," he said finally. A faint humor eased the corners of his mouth for a brief instant. "By now, I don't imagine that it is necessary to tell you that I am taking over command of CCB. I am glad to see you."

He saw no reflection of his humor in the eyes of the men who looked back at him. Their faces were either woodenly expressionless or clearly hostile. He'd expected a degree of this, but he hadn't expected to encounter a wall of resistance quite this solid and impenetrable. He abandoned the informal approach he'd meant to make. The devil with it; he'd make this strictly military. If that was the way they wanted it, that was the way they were going to get it!

"Introduce your officers, Colonel Nash," he said.

Already he knew the names of most of them. The rosters on the refectory table had told him that. After he'd managed to get down a half-can of K-ration Lute had brought, he'd spent the rest of the time before 2000 going over the rosters, strength returns, other reports.

There was Garton who commanded the armored infantry battalion; Ickles and Kowansky who had the two self-propelled 105-mm howitzer battalions; Cross of the armored engineer company; and O'Shiel of the tank destroyer company. Three or four others who had the medical company, the armored reconnaissance company, the antiaircraft artillery battery, and the armored maintenance company. Nash called off their names curtly.

As each was named he stepped forward, got his nod from Boone, then stepped back. Good enough looking soldiers, the back of Boone's mind was telling him. Good soldiers when they are pulling as a team — as they pulled for Martell. Not worth a hoot in the frame of mind they're in now. Well, it's up to me to snap them out of it and I've got a hunch I haven't much time to do it in. The last of them, Captain Hewitt, commanding the antiaircraft artillery battery, stepped back against the wall.

"Thank you," Boone said curtly. "I haven't got any pep talk for you, gentlemen. You lost a fine commander in General Martell. I intend to try to take his place. From you I will expect the same loyalty and performance you gave to him. Not more, but certainly not less. Are there any questions?"

There were none. It was growing colder in the kitchen as the fire began to die on the hearth. The hostile atmosphere that filled the room was colder still.

"Tomorrow, beginning at 1300, I will conduct a showdown inspection of the whole command," he continued. "The executive will furnish you a schedule of the time your units may expect me. The inspection will be thorough. If there are still no questions, that is all, gentlemen."

They filed out into the night and the cold rain. Just before the door closed on the last of them Miles heard a voice incautiously lifted. "Lousy

Pentagon general," it said. He shrugged and went back to work on the reports at the table.

He should have Nash and Summer and Jefferson and Potts in here to help him, Miles knew. Right now he didn't want them. He'd do this by himself. He was accustomed to paperwork, he thought grimly. He ought to be after four years at a desk! Then some sense began to take shape in the mass of papers and he forgot his dark forebodings as he began to unravel the complexities of Combat Command B.

He had not noticed the time — it was past midnight as he glanced at his watch. A door creaked faintly as it opened. Sergeant Lute Heard, he guessed, without turning his head.

"Go get in the sack where you belong, Lute," he said irritably. "Confound it, haven't you been in the Army long enough to know to sleep when you can?"

Janet de Ceilly's voice said gently behind him, "I'm afraid that I haven't been in the Army at all, General. You're working late. I thought perhaps you'd enjoy some coffee."

The rain had turned to snow during the night. As Miles Boone stepped outside the kitchen in the early dawn, the fields stretched away beneath capes of white. The powdery stuff which still fell had put caps on the firs along the Couteaux road so that they resembled solemn monks discussing the coming day. Sergeant Lute Heard came clumping up, sour with an old man's early morning crankiness. He grunted at Miles's "good morning."

"If I had the sense I was born with I'd still be back at Knox with another good hour of sacktime left an' nothing to worry about except left-footed recruits," Lute said glumly. "I wouldn't be here freezin' my fool self to death."

"If you had the sense you were born with you wouldn't be in the Army at all," Miles said good-humoredly. "Want me to arrange to have you ordered back, Lute? After all, you're getting along in years. It's a young man's war, I've heard."

Lute spat tobacco juice onto the new snow and gave Miles a venomous glance. "Any day I can't out-drink, out-cuss, and out-soldier anybody you can name, you let me know," he said crossly. "I located the headquarters mess — it's around the corner. Go get a cup of coffee. Maybe your disposition'll improve."

He tramped indignantly off through the snow and Miles chuckled a little as he watched him go. The black depression which had held him for a little while last night was gone now. Perhaps it was due to the cold air of the morning; perhaps it was because of the challenge of the day that lay ahead.

But that was not the whole reason, Miles Boone knew. All those things contributed to the good feeling that he had this morning, but they were just part of the good feeling that had carried over from last night. He and Janet de Ceilly had talked over their coffee for more than an hour after midnight.

They'd spoken of Dobbs Ferry and West Point;

they'd recalled how the hills above the Hudson had looked when they'd donned their scarlet and gold cloaks of autumn, and the picture that sailboats had made on the river; they had dwelt on dozens of things that he'd long ago forgotten but had come back with nostalgic clearness last night. They'd sipped coffee and talked with the casual ease of old friends. When they'd finally said good night, Miles had had the feeling that he'd known Janet for a long time.

At the door, he'd held her hand for a little longer than had been necessary; then he'd released it suddenly, flushing a little as he had realized that he had wanted to say good night in a warmer manner than this. A lot warmer manner. Well, Combat Command B should be here at Couteaux for another week yet — maybe ten days. There would still be time.

"For cripe's sake, go get that coffee, Boone," he said aloud to himself now. "Heard was right — you need it!"

Out in the white fields tank engines growled and backfired as tracks began to turn and drivers maneuvered the big machines into the shelter of the copse or of the buildings and dispersed those it was impossible to hide. The pristine carpet lost its freshness as clanking treads spewed up the mud beneath. The snow had changed to rain again, a slow drizzle which fell steadily.

Butch Marcus, shouting directions to his driver, worked his big Sherman beneath a cowshed, ousting a tank destroyer which had already taken shelter there. The tank destroyer sergeant yelled maledictions as he moved off to find a new place.

"Lousy tankers!" he yapped violently. "Who give you the idea you own the earth?"

Butch grinned complacently, leaning his arms on the rim of the hatch. "My, my, such language," he said. "You ought to have your mouth washed out with soap, Sergeant. What if your good pastor was to hear you?"

"My good pastor knows what he can do!" the tank destroyer sergeant retorted furiously. "The next time I go to any war it won't be with no tanker outfit, you can bet! You know what you can do, too!"

"Tch! Tch! How some folks do carry on," Butch said happily to Steve Reilly. "Well, let's get at that gun, boy. I got a hunch it ain't goin' to be no Sunday school inspection that our new general turns out this afternoon."

"That's the way I heerd it," Reilly agreed, unbothered. "Remind me to steal a helmet, Sarge. I wouldn't want to go to no inspection half nekkid."

"Where's your own helmet? You drew a new one last week, I seem to remember."

"Oh, that one," Reilly said, opening the breech of the tank gun and squinting critically through the barrel. "I lost it to a gal in Couteaux."

"What do you mean, you lost it?"

"Say I give it to her as a *sou*-venir," Reilly said. "Give me that rag."

Miles Boone was sitting at the table drinking coffee, Nash saw as he came into the small room which held the headquarters mess. Nash halted for a split second then started to back out again, but Boone stopped him.

"Come in, Colonel," Miles said, his voice impersonal and showing no trace in it of what had happened yesterday. "Sit down — have some coffee? I didn't ask you for those status reports last night because I had other things on my mind. You can give them to me now, if you will."

Nelson Nash's face was wooden as he sat down at the table and called for a cook to bring him coffee. He was thinking, though, I'll just bet that you had other things on your mind, General. A soldier, wearing a flour sack for an apron, brought the coffee and Nash took a slip of paper from the pocket of his shirt.

"Yes, sir," he said, his voice deferential. "I have the figures here. Which would you like first, sir?"

After the 2000 meeting last night, Nelson Nash — no fool when it came to the politics of the Army — had taken careful stock of the situation. He'd assessed it thoroughly, particularly its aspects as they might affect Nelson Nash. You didn't openly buck a general, he knew; not if you wanted to keep your neck out of a high sling. Blood had a habit of running down your shirt front in the Army; it didn't run up. That was axiomatic.

He'd heard the rumor that Miles Boone wasn't in too well with Major General Clark Blocker, the division commander, and he'd look a little further into that. A man could learn a lot if he dropped over to division headquarters now and then and kept his eyes and ears open. Besides that, he had a couple of good friends there; they'd be glad to keep him posted on things. Meanwhile, he'd just play it cozy here at Combat Command B and wait for Boone to stub his toe. It was bound to happen sooner or later. And when it did, Nelson Nash meant to make the most of it.

"Tank strength," Boone said in answer to Nash's question. "First mediums — then lights."

"We're 85 per cent effective in the mediums," Nash said, reading aloud from the slip in his hand. "We've got 90 per cent of our lights, General."

"Break down the ones we haven't got."

Again Nash consulted the paper. The commanding officer of the armored regiment should have those facts etched in his mind, Miles thought disapprovingly. He shouldn't have to consult a slip of paper in order to find them. The unfavorable impression he'd gotten of Nash last night was not improved.

"Ten of the mediums are in the shop undergoing repair or modification. The same for four of the lights. The rest are replacement vehicles we haven't received yet."

Miles tucked the figures away in his mind — then asked abruptly, "Why haven't we received them, Colonel? The combat command has been here long enough for new tanks to come all of the way from England, confound it!"

Nash shrugged. "I've requisitioned them, sir. The

ordnance people back in Com Zee are just slow, I guess."

"All right," Boone said curtly, "after we finish here, Colonel, get yourself a truck and some drivers and go after those tanks. I want them here by this time tomorrow!"

The color deepened in Nash's face and for a moment resentment showed in his eyes. "Just how do I get them, General?"

"Jacob's teeth, *I* don't care how you get them!" Boone said, temper flaring. "Steal them! Ask Eisenhower for them! Take it up with Roosevelt if you have to — just get them! And I want those cripples out of the repair shop by tomorrow, too! How about personnel? How do we stand there?"

Nash, a little shaken, consulted his slip again. "The combat command as a whole is up to about 95 per cent of Table of Organization strength, sir," he said. "I understand that fifty more replacements, chiefly for the armored infantry battalion, are due to arrive here today."

"Good," Boone grunted. "Ammunition?"

"All vehicles have their combat loads, sir."

"Not bad except for the tanks," Miles said, finishing his coffee and getting to his feet. "I'll expect you to have that situation in hand by noon tomorrow, Nash. See you later."

Lieutenant Colonel Ike Garton, commanding the armored infantry battalion, had his command post in what had been a small guest cottage. He sat in a chair tipped against the wall, his feet on a table, while he talked with Major Stan Kowansky, who had one of the field artillery battalions, and Dennis O'Shiel, who ran the tank destroyer company. Garton was a tall, lanky man with a mournful face and a drooping mustache. When he moved, he seemed to move in sections like the unfolding of a carpenter's rule.

"We'll make out," he was saying in his undertaker's voice. "The infantry ain't all gowed up with gadgets like you smart specialists are. Rifle, ammo, helmet and first-aid packet — that's all we got to have and we're ready to go to war. A showdown inspection don't worry us none, brothers."

Major Kowansky took off his glasses and wiped them, peering with an anxious nearsightedness out of the window. He'd been a bookkeeper before the war and he liked things to be neat and orderly and to add up like a column of figures.

"I don't know," he said. "Maybe it would have been all right with General Martell. With this new general just out from the Pentagon I just don't know. He's liable to be particular about little things. Like, has each of your men got an extra pair of bootlaces? I was up half the night finding extra bootlaces for the battalion. Do you see what I mean?"

Denny O'Shiel, as lanky as Garton but not as tall, rolled a brown-paper cigarette from sack tobacco, a habit left over from his cowboy days in Texas. "Shoelaces — what are them?" he asked in his lazy drawl. "My boys don't need 'em. Remember when we were next to that Air Corps field back in Sep-

tember? We high-graded enough Air Corps boots
to last us if this war goes on to a year from Christmas. You never saw such a mad bunch of fly-boys
in your life," he added, slapping his leg and laughing silently.

"Just the same, you'd better have shoelaces,"
Kowansky persisted in his worried voice. "I *hear*
that General Boone has already jumped all over
Colonel Nash and the staff. We're next, you mark
my words."

"Let him jump," Garton said, looking sadder than
ever. "I'm used to it, I've had some real experts
jump over me, pal. As for that fat Summer, what-
ever he got he had coming in my book. The same
goes for Nellie Nash."

"I don't know about Major Summer," Kowansky
said worriedly, putting his glasses back on. "I think
you're wrong about Colonel Nash, Ike. He's always
been a gentleman to me."

"Yeah, yeah," Garton said. "Like butter wouldn't
melt in his mouth. Well, I ain't no prophet but I got
a hunch that before long we're going to be back in
a fight right up to our necks. And in a fight you
don't want no gentleman telling you what to do,
brother. You want a tough, mean, German-killing
man, see? And I have a hunch that that's what we
got."

O'Shiel stood up, yawning. "Hope that hunch of
yours don't pan out, Ike," he said.

"I still say you'd better check on the bootlaces,"
Kowansky said. "He's sure to ask about them."

Miles Boone was at work in the kitchen when the phone from division rang at midmorning. Leroy Jefferson took the call. Miles was studying a map, his forehead wrinkled as he went over the road net to the south and east. All morning the premonition had been growing in him that trouble was about to break somewhere along the Ghost Front. The Germans were sure to know how thinly that line was held. The German position was desperate. What was more likely than that Hitler should take a last wild gamble where the Americans were least expecting it? What had he to lose? Such an action was in keeping with everything else he had done in this war.

Boone looked up to see Jefferson beside him. "It's General Blocker on the line, sir," Jefferson said. "He wants to talk to you about those tanks. He sounds mad."

Miles took the phone. "Boone speaking," he said.

Clark Blocker's voice grated in his ear. "What do you mean by sending Nash out to steal tanks?" the other demanded wrathfully. "Is that your idea of running a combat command?"

Three

MILES BOONE'S FACE DARKENED A LITTLE as he stood holding the handset of the field telephone to his ear and listening to Major General Clark Blocker's harsh voice blast him over the wire. He'd sent Colonel Nelson Nash out to do a job, he was thinking, and the first thing that Nash had done was to run complaining to the division commander. Then Boone's face relaxed a little and his lips lifted over his even teeth in a wry grin.

You told him to get those tanks in any way he could, Miles, he was thinking a little ruefully. You can hardly scream foul when Nash went to division for them.

"I'm waiting for an answer, Boone," Blocker was saying roughly. "Just what do you mean by sending Nash up here to heckle my G-4 about your tanks?"

"I'm short those tanks," Miles said evenly. "I want them and I mean to get them. I told Nash to go clear back to Paris to get them if he had to. Those orders still stand."

Some of the bluster suddenly went out of Clark Blocker's voice but Boone had a clear picture of the other, sitting behind his polished desk, eyes a little narrowed as he talked. Waiting for me to make that first mistake, he thought. This isn't it — it's not big enough. And I still mean to have those tanks.

"You wouldn't be trying to go over my head, would you, General?" Blocker asked now, his voice faintly curious. "I've figured you for a lot of things. That wasn't one of them."

"I'm not trying anything," Miles said smothering his impatience. "I simply want those tanks and I want them soon."

"Why? What's the rush?"

"All right, General," Boone said bluntly, "because I've got a feeling that something big is about to break on the Our. If that happens, we'll be mixed up in it. Combat Command B is not going into a fight without its full complement of armor if I can help it. That's the whole of it!"

He expected Blocker's angry voice to blast him off the phone. It didn't. The other end was silent for a moment; then, when he spoke again, Major General Clark Blocker's tone was strangely thoughtful.

"So, you've been looking at the map, too, have you?" he asked. "You've been looking at the same place I have. Maybe you have seen the same thing . . . the high-priced Intelligence experts we've got in this business notwithstanding . . ."

Blocker's voice trailed off at the other end of the line and, for a moment, Miles thought that the other had hung up. Then the voice came back, even more brusque now.

"All right, Boone," it said. "Only, if you lock

horns with some rear area big-shot over poking your nose into his business, don't come crying to me. I can't quarrel with a commander because he wants his equipment. I'm still warning you, though — you're allowed just one mistake. Just one."

He hung up then and Miles put down the handset. Major Summer bustled in with his hands full of papers and his manner full of importance. This morning he had shaved so closely that his face looked as though it had been peeled, Boone noted with mild amusement. Major Frank Summer had seen the handwriting on the wall and had interpreted it correctly, he guessed.

"What have you there, Major?" he asked.

"Recreation schedules, sir," Summer said, all efficiency. "With Christmas less than two weeks away, I thought I'd better get them checked up. I've arranged for a USO outfit to be here and we'll have a big Christmas tree in the courtyard and . . ."

"That's fine, Major," Miles agreed absently as his uneasy forebodings began to ride him again. "Let's just hope that we're still around here when Christmas Day comes."

It was dusk, the drizzle turning to snow again, when Miles Boone, Lute Heard with him, finished the showdown inspection. Miles was tired and his muscles ached from climbing in and out of tanks, stooping to peer beneath half-tracks, checking other types of vehicles and the weapons that went with them, moving slowly along lines of men where personal equipment was laid out for inspection.

Major Stanley Kowansky's prediction had not come true. The question of extra bootlaces had not been raised.

Other things had.

Were tank guns clean — recoil cylinders filled? Was ammunition properly stowed? Ninety-seven rounds for the 75-mm cannon; 4,750 rounds, armor piercing and tracer, for the .30 caliber machine guns; three hundred rounds for the .50 caliber guns; six hundred rounds of caliber .45 for the tommy guns; ten grenades, fragmentation, smoke, incendiary. Were the radios working and the motors tuned?

Details. Minutiae. Things too small for a general to concern himself with? Yet they were the nails without which the shoe is lost — hence the battle. The details that might be a matter of life or death later on.

Sergeant Butch Marcus spat philosophically after Boone had left his tank, named — with a nice touch of sentiment, so Butch considered — the *Fayetteville Floozy*. He watched Miles depart with a thoughtful eye and then spoke to Reilly.

"For a guy who's been sittin' at a desk," he said, "he knows plenty about tanks, thank you kindly, ma'am. Considering he's a general, he is downright intelligent at times."

"So what?" Reilly asked. He was wearing the crash helmet he'd borrowed from a tanker in another company when the latter wasn't looking. "He has to know something to earn his pay, don't he? Why not know about tanks?"

"Why not, indeed?" Butch echoed. "It's more'n

our Nellie knows. Once back in France Nellie is snoopin' around the *Floozy*. He climbs up on the hull and pokes his nose down the hatch.

" 'What is that, Sergeant?' he wants to know, pointin' to the sight periscope with his pinky.

" 'The periscope, sir,' I says.

" 'Oh, yes, the periscope,' he says. 'Uh, for crossing rivers, I suppose.'

" 'Yes, sir,' I say, not battin' an eye. 'Them rivers shore can get awful deep, Colonel.' "

"That's our Nellie," Reilly agreed. "You don't catch him getting all greasy climbing around in no tanks. When they were passing out brains, he must of been goofing off somewhere else. Well, let's get this tin can buttoned up and shag tail for the chow line. It's about that time."

It was no accident that Miles Boone knew tanks and everything that fought with tanks. Armor was the new cavalry in this war and he was a cavalryman. He'd learned about tanks first on the antiquated vehicles of the First Armored Brigade back in 1939 and 1940. Clumsy stuff, but a beginning.

Then, during those four long years in Washington, after he'd put in his seemingly endless hours at a desk, Miles Boone had burned the midnight oil seven days a week in his cramped bachelor apartment poring over manuals, blueprints, diagrams, drawings. He'd spent his weekends, when he could get away, watching tanks and gun carriages and fire control instruments being made. He'd bootlegged trips to the training centers where he'd gotten his knowledge of the tools of an armored division at firsthand, doing the chores himself. He had learned thoroughly and well.

It had been this study and preparation that had really kept him sane during those maddening months in the War Department. Now it was paying off, he thought with a faint satisfaction as he tramped back through the snow towards the farmhouse kitchen. The cold dusk was beginning to come down.

"I seen worse outfits," Lute Heard said beside him.

"It's a good outfit," Miles said. "With a few days to get it up into the collar again, it'll be ready. God grant that we've got those few days."

"That Our business still buggin' you?"

"You could say that," Miles answered.

"Me, I'm an optimist," Lute said, spitting tobacco juice into the snow. "I figure that between Santy Claus an' Franklin Roosevelt we got this war about over."

"I hope you're right," Miles told him absently. "But I wouldn't bet on it if I were you."

As darkness came down east of the Our River, a thousand German units began their final inching movements up to the lines of departure from which they would jump off at dawn. It was the night of December 15. Tomorrow Operation Christrose would begin. Tomorrow was the day. The great day. *Der Tag!*

Radios were silent so that no intercepted message would give away the assault. Tank engines were mute. Only the infantry moved. As German soldiers assembled in their forward positions, their officers read them a personal message from Field Marshal Gerd von Rundstedt.

SOLDIERS OF THE WESTERN FRONT! YOUR GREAT HOUR HAS COME! WE GAMBLE EVERYTHING! YOU CARRY WITH YOU THE HOLY OBLIGATION TO GIVE ALL . . . FOR OUR FATHERLAND AND OUR FÜHRER!

And in Krinkelt and Losheimergraben and Krewinkel and Winterspelt there still was no cause for Allied alarm. G.I.s drank beer or talked with the local girls or went to a movie. Some of them slept. At Bastogne, corps headquarters went about its business undisturbed by the storm brewing to the east. At Combat Command B, men talked of the showdown inspection that had been held that afternoon.

"It was a doozey," Willie Murch, a rifleman in the armored infantry battalion, said. "Yup, a doozey."

"You can say that again," his listener agreed. "I thought Martell was tough — I guess we ain't seen nothing yet."

Colonel Nelson Nash was back by midmorning on the 16th. He had the tanks. Not all of them but almost all and it was enough to satisfy Miles Boone, who stood in the muddy snow and watched as the big machines clanked by. A mud-spattered staff car turned out of the column and stopped. Nash climbed stiffly down and came to meet Miles.

The colonel's eyes were red from sleeplessness and his once immaculate uniform was stained with oil and snagged from climbing in and out of tank hatches.

"Well, there's your tanks," he said in a tone of voice that Miles hadn't heard before. "All I could get. Don't ask me where or how I got them — a court-martial would give me a thousand years for the things that I've done in the last twenty-four hours! I wouldn't blame it!"

"You've done a good job, Nash," Miles said quietly. "Get some sleep — you've earned it. If anyone comes around talking about a court-martial, it's me they'll have to talk to."

Nash gave Miles a swift glance out of the corner of his eye and, for a brief instant, a puzzled shadow crossed his unshaven face. Then he turned without a word and climbed back into the muddy staff car. He'd done things yesterday and today that had surprised even himself, he was thinking. And he had a little warm feeling in him for having done them. Now, why was that, he wondered? Tiredness and no breakfast, he supposed.

It was past noon and Miles was at the gun park of one of the field artillery battalions when Captain Potts found him — the general was to call Major General Clark Blocker at division headquarters right away. It was important.

"He still sounds mad," Captain Potts added, looking at Boone owlishly. "I tried to take the message, sir."

"Thanks," Miles said. "I'm used to him, son."

This chubby captain, Jeremiah Potts, was beginning to grow on him, he decided as he turned back towards the farmhouse. His mind went on to the impending call. Somebody has missed some tanks, he thought wryly. It didn't take them long to yell. Well, here we go again.

Oddly enough, as he went through the snow, the possibility that this call could be connected with the surprise assault he had predicted didn't occur to Miles Boone. He was still thinking of tanks as he entered the farmhouse, picked up the handset, and told the switchboard operator to get General Blocker on the line. There was a wait that stretched out into minutes before Clark Blocker's voice, harsh and angry, finally answered.

"This is Boone," Miles said.

"All right," Blocker said bluntly. "It seems that we were both right in what we thought might break loose down south. We've reports — none clear yet — that something is going on down there. It could be just a little spoiling attack. It could be something a lot bigger. My guess is the latter. The division has orders to move to Rigny as soon as possible. That's roughly seventy-five kilometers southeast of here."

"I know where it is on the map," Miles said.

Blocker's voice became more edged. "Good! Combat Command B will move out first. How soon can you be on the road?"

"In two hours," Miles said.

It wasn't a snap judgment, Boone knew. Subconsciously he had been anticipating this since he'd studied that map last night. The showdown inspection in the afternoon had confirmed his estimate as to CCB's readiness and his plans were already made. The arrival of Nash with the extra tanks today had been all that was needed to wrap the thing up.

Now there was a silence at the other end of the line — then Blocker's voice came back, disbelieving. "I've just been checking. The rest of the division won't be able to move out before midnight. Yet you say you can move in two hours. Do you expect me to believe that?"

"I do," Boone said curtly.

Again silence. Then Blocker said, his voice formal and cold, "You'd better not be grandstanding, Boone. You've said that you can be on the road in two hours — in exactly two hours I'll expect a report from you that you're moving. Pick your own route. It's likely that there'll be a lot of other stuff on the road. I don't know what the situation is at Rigny. Take over there until I arrive. Do you understand?"

"I understand," Miles said.

It was 1410 when Boone reported to division that Combat Command B was on the road; the two hours were up, to the minute. He stood in the new snow that had started to fall and watched the elements as they passed. The reconnaissance company, scout cars well out in the van, headed the march column.

Now the armored regiment came, the big Sher-

mans lumbering by, tracks clanking and engines
roaring — tank commanders standing in the turrets.
The armored infantry in half-tracks, men huddled
together against the cold, but perversely happy —
as is the way of soldiers — to be on the move
again. Even though it meant, as it probably did,
that they were on their way into a new battle. It
had that virtue, at least. It was new.

The self-propelled battalions went by, muzzle
covers on the artillery tubes, tarps tied down over
the guns. Scattered along throughout the column
were the Quad 50s of the antiaircraft artillery, the
four barrels tilted to the sky despite the fact that
there was little to fear from the air in this weather.
The column rumbled on. Armored engineers and
the tank destroyer company and the medical company and the maintenance people. . . .

A small thrill of pride ran through Miles Boone
as he watched them go by. This was the moment
he had been building towards when he'd first
climbed that long hill from the railroad station to
West Point those long years ago. This was the best
moment the world could offer a soldier: that moment when he led other men towards battle. There
was no other like it.

Sergeant Heard brought up the jeep, a radio
operator riding in back, and parked a few yards
away. Miles motioned for him to wait as he turned
back towards the farmhouse kitchen. He knew,
somehow, that Janet would be standing there waiting for him just inside the doorway. For a moment
neither spoke.

Janet said then, "It's been such a short time, hasn't it, Miles? So very short."

"That's the way war is, Janet," Miles heard himself saying. He'd meant just to say good-bye, but now his words seemed to be spilling out of their own accord. "I guess that's why I've got to do it this way — there's so little time. Janet, after all of this is over, will you marry me?"

She said, "Of course," and came into his arms.

They stood for a moment; then Miles released her gently. He stood in the doorway looking at her as though he must remember the smallest detail of this moment. Then he was gone, looking back no more. He moved through the snow with purposeful strides until he reached the jeep; his face showed no emotion as he climbed into the front seat beside Lute Heard.

"Get to the head of the column," he said.

Lute put the vehicle into gear and stepped on the throttle; they went through the gate of the courtyard and the jeep lurched and bucked as Heard took a short cut across the hummocky fields. His weathered face was impassive but he glanced now and then at Miles Boone out of the corner of his eye. Wisely he made no mention of the scene back at the farmhouse.

Heard said presently, "I ain't got around to askin' — we headed for the Our, Miles?"

"That's right."

"Nuts," Lute said mournfully after a moment. "I should have knowed better than to believe in Santy

Claus — let alone Franklin Roosevelt. Well, that's the way it goes."

The column left the dirt road and turned south on the main highway three miles east of Couteaux. At Boone's grunted order, Lute again pulled the jeep off the road, where Miles checked the march discipline as the column passed. It was good. Vehicles were holding their distances and the pace was steady. A fierce pride in Combat Command B was growing in him.

Maybe CCB had grown a little lax, a little slovenly, back there in its rest billets at the farm. Now that it was moving toward battle again it had sluffed off its lazy indifference as a snake sheds its skin. It marched with an assured competence, alert and combat-wise.

"Let's get up front again," Boone said.

They rode at the head of the armored regiment, the recon company with its scout cars flung out ahead of them, Boone studying the map spread on his knees as they went. They were following the main highway running south from Liège; a sign, back where they had entered the road, had read BASTOGNE — 68 KILOMETERS. Traffic was not heavy. The map showed that another road, running east and west, intersected this one ten kilometers farther along. The crossroads was named Saint Heye.

The column would turn east there, Boone decided. It would cross the Vaar River at Vaaracre; then it would take the road running southeast to Rigny, a half dozen miles west of the Our. At its present march rate, CCB should close in Rigny by about twenty-one hundred hours, but he wasn't too sanguine about that. If the Germans had made any sort of a breakthrough it was likely that the roads would be clogged with stragglers and refugees once Combat Command B had crossed the Vaar. Its pace could be slowed down to a crawl. Well, he'd worry about that when he came to it.

He said over his shoulder to the radio operator riding in the rear of the jeep, "Tell Lieutenant Dunn I want to see him, son," and heard the operator calling softly into his mike.

First Lieutenant Helvar Dunn, commanding the armored recon company, was parked on the shoulder of the road as Boone's jeep drew abreast. Dunn's driver expertly jockeyed his own vehicle alongside and Dunn stepped across the gap to crouch beside the radio operator while he peered over Boone's shoulder.

"We turn east here at Saint Heye crossroads," Boone said, pointing on the map. "Go southeast on this road once we cross the Vaar. Better mark your map."

"Got it, sir," Dunn said.

He was a tall, square-built youth with Scandinavian blood showing in his fair skin and blond hair. Boone glanced back at him — started to give the boy instructions about the road control at Saint Heye and the reconnaissance towards Vaaracre. Then he decided that he wouldn't. Something in Dunn's poised manner and the steadiness of his pale blue eyes said that it wasn't necessary. Miles liked that. The boy knew his job; he'd give him a chance to do it, he thought as he turned back.

"Okay, Dunn," he said. "It's your baby. Keep us rolling — that's all I ask. If you run into something too big for you to handle, don't be afraid to yell for help."

"We'll keep rolling, General."

Dunn transferred to his own jeep with an agility surprising in a big man. Tires screeched as the other vehicle leaped ahead, weaving in and out of the column, and disappeared over a rise ahead. The snow had stopped but low-hanging clouds, gray and somber as the caps of prison towers, promised that it would soon fall again. The wind was so cold that Boone hunched his shoulders against its bite as he rode.

"This day has got a feel to it I don't like," Lute Heard said morosely. "You think the Germans have really bruk through, Miles? I thought they was all washed up."

"You've fought Germans before," Miles said. "You ought to know how mean they can get just when you think you've got them licked. This could be one of those times."

"I was afraid you were goin' to say that," Lute answered in a glum voice. "I should have kept my big mouth shut while I was still ahead."

It was a little after 1500 when the recon company rolled through Saint Heye and turned east. Not much to the place, Boone noted. A stone château, with its outbuildings, stood here on ground which rose slightly above a marshland ringed with firs. A half dozen nondescript civilians stood in the snow to watch the column pass, showing neither hostility nor enthusiasm as they watched. If they had heard of a German breakthrough they did not show it, either by action or manner.

Helvar Dunn waved a scout car out of column to take station here and make sure that each following echelon made its proper turn, Boone noted with satisfaction. He had been right. The boy knew his job. The combat command was strung out now with transient vehicles from other outfits crowded into the gaps and it would be easy for a following unit to miss the change of direction and keep heading south towards Bastogne. Traffic had thickened on the Liège highway but there was little going east on the Vaaracre road, Boone noted.

The afternoon was dying fast as they came into Vaaracre an hour and a half later. Miles Boone was partially prepared for what he found in this small town huddled on the west bank of the river. For the past half hour the column had been running into increasingly heavier straggler traffic moving towards the west — none of it sure where it was going or what had happened. Vaaracre was a crazy confusion of such traffic — mainly personnel and vehicles from service units — and flotsam that had drifted back when the German offensive exploded out of the fog in the morning.

Boone waved Dunn and the recon company across the bridge over the Vaar, then left the radio operator to guard the jeep while he went on foot through the town to pick up what information he could. Few knew anything, he found. He finally collared a lost and scared lieutenant who wore the ordnance device.

"What's your outfit?" Boone snapped.

The lieutenant named a medium maintenance company, stuttering a little as he spoke, his eyes like those of a sleepwalker. They'd been camped a little east of Rigny last night, he said. Nobody had told them that anything was about to happen. They'd gone to bed . . .

"Get on with it," Miles said curtly.

Okay. Okay. They'd been wakened this morning by shelling. A lot of shelling. German stuff coming from beyond the Our. At first they hadn't paid too much attention; the shells hadn't been falling close. Then, just as they were lining up for breakfast, German tanks were right in their laps! How many? A dozen — maybe a hundred! Big, wicked-looking devils with guns spitting and black crosses painted on their sides! They'd run right over the company . . .

"Where's your company now, Lieutenant?" Boone interrupted sharply. "Here in Vaaracre?"

The lieutenant ran a dirty hand over his face and licked his lips vaguely. "I don't know, General," he said, his voice indifferent and thick with shock. "I've got six men with me — we got here in a truck. The rest could be anywhere. Maybe dead."

Boone got the same story, with variations, from half a dozen others. Nobody knew for sure what had happened. They'd looked up and the Germans had been in their laps; their units had disintegrated. They'd drifted back along the Vaaracre road and now they were here. Miles listened and noted the places on his map, and he knew that this was no spoiling attack. This was a breakthrough and it was big. Bigger even than he had imagined it would be.

"Step on it," he said to Lute Heard as they got back to the jeep. "We've got our troubles from now on."

"I wouldn't argue with you," Lute said sourly. "I've seen my share of foul-ups in this man's Army, but it sure looks like we got a jim-dandy this time."

Fog hung heavy and gray over the eighty miles of the Ghost Front as the day of December 16th reluctantly dawned. There was no real dawn, only a lessening of the blackness of the night so that, little by little, dark fir clusters began to take shape on the snow-covered hills and moving shadows slowly acquired the reality of men. A whisper ran through the fog. A strong whisper that started at Monschau and followed the line to Echternach eighty miles away. A whisper that seemed to set loose the lightning and thunder.

"All batteries ready!"

"All batteries . . . fire!"

At five-thirty on a foggy morning, the battle day of December 16th began. Operation Christrose. *Der Tag.* When the day ended, the whole of the Ardennes was aflame. It was no great set battle piece like the charge of Pickett's gray legions at Gettysburg. It was a battle made up of a thousand tiny fights, each waged with the ferocity of a Waterloo.

It was a battle of a thousand small heroisms and a thousand small cowardices. Above all, it was a battle of confusion. Part of the confusion was planned — jeeploads of German soldiers, dressed in American uniforms, roamed the countryside in front of the panzer spearheads, surprising command posts, disrupting communications, issuing false orders that compounded panic.

Late in the afternoon of the 16th one of these phony officers in an American jeep came to the command post of a United States infantry regiment in the schoolhouse at Rigny.

"Take me to your commanding officer," the lieutenant said sharply to the sergeant of the security guard. He spoke with the accent of South Chicago. "Immediately, soldier!"

"Yes, sir," the sergeant said. "Lootenant, what's goin' on up front? We been hearin' . . ."

"The Germans have broken through," the lieutenant said. "The whole front has caved in. I've got orders for your colonel that the regiment is to retire at once . . ."

"Holy smoke!" the sergeant said.

He was green. His division had not been there long and it had not seen battle before. It did not take much time for the word to spread and it got worse with each telling. Fifty kilometers away, east of the Vaar, Combat Command B, Hammerhead Armored Division, slowed to a walk as it bucked stragglers.

There was plenty of traffic on the road now, Miles Boone noted grimly as Lute zigzagged the jeep in and out of the column. Precious little of it, except for CCB, was moving towards the east. Westbound traffic was rapidly thickening — a motley assortment of vehicles moving in headlong flight without order and without discipline. Supply trucks, ambulances, staff cars, jeeps, repair vans, were all crowded with muddy, wild-eyed men.

Most of the command had crossed the Vaar while Boone had been searching for information in Vaaracre. Now Lute jockeyed the jeep with all of the cunning at his command as he tried to get back to the head of the column. They came up to the rear of one of the armored field artillery battalions. It was stalled on the road, unable to move because of the jam ahead.

"We've got to get through," Boone said sharply.

"Hang on," Lute grunted.

They skidded on the slick shoulder of the road. Heard slid the jeep through openings where the clearance was paper-thin. Engine roaring, he jinked in and out, cutting in front of traffic going west, disregarding other drivers who swore and shook their fists at him. In the back of the jeep the radio operator hung on, a frozen grin on his freckled face. Combat Command B's column was completely stalled now and Boone knew that he had to get it rolling again and do it fast. Less than an hour of daylight remained and Rigny was still twenty miles ahead.

They finally came up to the recon company again and Lute brought the jeep to a stop as Boone saw what the trouble was. A large machine-shop truck had stalled, blocking half of the road; other vehicles jammed the road solidly from shoulder to shoulder behind the obstacle while a trickle flowed by it to the rear. Dunn was in the cab with the driver of the stalled shop truck, vainly trying to get it started again.

"Take me back to the lead tank," Miles snapped to Lute, sliding into the seat again. "Fast!"

It wasn't far and it was Butch Marcus' tank, Butch standing in the turret with his padded helmet pushed to the back of his head and his eyes bright and observant. Boone jumped from the jeep to the hull of the *Fayetteville Floozy* as Butch watched. Until now he had remained pretty neutral regarding this guy from Washington, Butch was thinking; what happened next was going to go a long ways towards confirming or disproving his opinion of generals, he decided. As of now it wasn't too high.

"Sergeant," Miles asked, his voice deceptively mild, "is your driver pretty good?"

Butch spat and rearranged the grease on his dirty face with a big paw. "General," he said, "all the guys I got in this tin can is good. I wouldn't have 'em if they weren't."

"Good," Miles snapped. "We're going to Rigny. Now! This minute! Move up ahead and shove that stalled machine-shop truck into the ditch. Then keep right on going. You understand? If anybody gets in your way, run over him!"

"General," Butch said, pleased, "we'll do that. Yes, sir, we'll shore do that! Hey, Pole, you hear?"

"I hear," the muffled voice of the driver said.

"Oh, another thing," Boone added. "I'll ride with you. Lend me your tommy gun, will you, Sergeant?"

Well, now, Butch was thinking, more pleased as he handed out the loaded submachine gun, maybe we got something going for us after all. Maybe this could be a little bit of all right.

The engine growled and the thirty-ton tank lurched forward. A battered jeep, filled with men, tried to dispute the right of way — too late they saw that the tank wasn't going to stop and skidded off the shoulder into the ditch, the driver howling maledictions. The tank came to where the machine-shop truck was stalled and Boone waved Helvar Dunn out of the cab. The tank driver nosed the bow of the big Sherman against the flank of the truck, gunned his engine and the clumsy repair vehicle went over with a crash.

The Sherman plowed on, gathering speed, and the hodgepodge collection of straggler vehicles scattered before it. Behind it the column was moving again, vehicles closed up bumper to bumper to form a solid battering ram of steel. Word ran ahead to traffic streaming down the road from Rigny.

"For the love of Mike, clear the road! There's a crazy general coming on a tank!"

Now the rear-going traffic was cautiously eased over onto its own side of the road, hugging the shoulder. But the word had not passed back far enough for a staff car that came bucketing suddenly around a bend, doubling the other column. It stopped with a squeal of brakes as it sighted the advancing tank. A staff colonel, wearing a natty trench coat, popped down into the road and came running forward. His voice was shrill with rage.

"Get those tanks out of the way!" he yelled at a muddy man, crouched on the lead tank's hull with a tommy gun in his hands. "I'm Colonel Murchinson of the . . ."

The tommy gun came up to stare him in the eye. "You'll be the late colonel if you don't get that car out of my way," Boone said coldly. "Driver . . ."

"I know," the driver said, his voice coming from the open driving hatch. "Run over the . . . !"

The staff car slid into the ditch and Combat Command B went on. Inside the turret, Butch Marcus hunkered down beside Reilly. "Don't look now," he said, yelling to make himself heard above the racket of the engine, "but I think we got ourselves a boy, Stevie. Yessir, I reely do!"

"Better'n Nellie?"

"Better'n Nellie," Butch said with satisfaction. "If Nellie was still runnin' this outfit we'd be back there with that stalled ordnance truck while he quoted Army regulations at the driver, I bet. I shouldn't wonder if I didn't get to almost like this new general we got."

"Well, I wouldn't go telling it around," Reilly said. "You got your reputation to think about."

"I wouldn't tell it to no one but you," Butch said. "From the looks of these heroes high-tailin' it to the rear, it might just be that we're goin' to get a bellyful of fightin' before this hooraw is over."

"Okay by me," Reilly said. "I love to fight. I come from a fighting family. The only time my old man and my old lady ever stopped fighting with each other was when it was time to eat. They were holy terrors, pal."

"I never knew you had any folks," Butch grunted. "I always figured they found you under a beer barrel."

He straightened and poked his head out of the turret again. The column was making better time now, but it still wasn't much more than a fast trot. The straggler vehicles were edged carefully over on their own side of the road; the passengers in these vehicles rode in a glum silence. Occasionally some soul more hardy than the rest would call a greeting.

"Where you going, tankers?"

"Up front. Where you think we're going?"

"You'll be sor . . . reee."

Boone waved to Lute Heard to bring the jeep alongside again. To Butch he said, "I'll keep the loan of your tommy gun a little longer. I'm leaving you now. Keep shoving."

"Yes, sir, General," Butch said with relish. "If they don't get out of the way, I run over 'em!"

"Check," Miles said.

He dropped to the jeep, catching the radio operator's steadying hand. At his word, Lute turned the jeep and they moved back down the column until they came to the tank in which Nelson Nash was riding. Boone scrambled onto the hull and hauled himself to where Nash stood in the turret.

"I'm taking Dunn and a scout car and going on ahead to Rigny," he said, shouting to make himself heard. "The situation there must be bad — I want to know what it is. Bring the command on as fast as you can, Nash."

The colonel looked back, poker-faced in the fading light. Snow had started again and the flakes melted on Boone's face, drops of water trickling from the point of his chin. He wiped at it impatiently as he waited for Nash's answer.

"That won't be fast," Nash said finally. "These stragglers are getting worse and . . ."

"I can think of a million reasons why it won't be fast," Boone said grimly. "I want Combat Command B in Rigny by midnight. You get it there, Colonel! That's all!"

He dropped back into the jeep. "Get going," he said. Lute Heard gunned the engine.

Helvar Dunn in the scout car cleared the way and the jeep followed. Boone had the map spread out on his knee again, hanging onto the crash bar with one hand while he squinted at the map symbols in the last of the light. Rigny shouldn't be far ahead, he reasoned. The intersecting road net showed that the place was important; that was the reason that the Hammerhead Division was being shoved up here, he knew. The town lay a half dozen miles west of the Our River and roads fed into it from the south, the east and the northeast. If the Germans had driven across the Our, Rigny would be one of the places they wanted.

They climbed a rise and started downhill again. At the far side of a shallow valley was a town, indistinctly seen through the snow and the growing darkness. It had to be Rigny, Miles knew. He could hear a low grumble far to the east now like the sound of distant thunder; it wasn't thunder — it was gunfire. Ahead of them Dunn's scout car stopped and the jeep pulled up beside it as Miles saw what blocked the way.

A tank destroyer sat in the middle of the road, the eye of its 90-mm gun staring at Miles as he stepped out of the jeep and went forward, Lute behind him. A sergeant with a tommy gun came from behind the tank destroyer, eying Boone and Heard suspiciously as he waited for them to come up.

"Who won the World Series?" he barked.

"A cockeyed joker," Lute said to Boone sourly under his breath. "That's all we need right now."

"Challenge properly, soldier!" Boone snapped, continuing to move forward. "I'm General Boone, commanding the . . ."

"I don't care if you're Moses off the mountain,"

the sergeant said grimly and the safety was removed on the submachine gun with an ominous click. "You ain't coming no nearer until you tell me who won the World Series."

"St. Louis," Miles said.

"Who lost it?"

"St. Louis. The Browns."

"Who won the Kentucky Derby?"

It was Lute Heard who answered. "Pensive," he said. "I ought to know — I had ten bucks bet on another nag."

The sergeant lowered the tommy gun. "I guess you're okay," he said grudgingly. "I'm sorry, General, everything has gone to heck in a hand basket around here, what with Germans running around in G.I. uniforms and riding American trucks and raising every kind of mischief you can put a name to. A phony lootenant showed up here in a jeep a couple of hours ago and told the Old Man to shag it out fast and . . ."

"Who's in command here?" Boone interrupted curtly.

"Colonel Brazos, sir," the sergeant said. He was glad to see company and wanted to talk. "He wouldn't buy this lootenant's story so we got the lootenant and the rest locked up, but things is sure a mess just the same with . . ."

"Where's his command post?"

"In the schoolhouse the other side of town. You can't miss it, General. It's a . . ."

"Wait here," Miles said to Dunn. To Lute he said, "Come on," and led the way back to the jeep.

It was dark now and the headlights bored palely into the falling snow as Lute took the jeep along the narrow and cobbled street. Stragglers were thicker here than they had been in Vaaracre. They filled the street, milling about like cattle. The houses thinned and Miles saw a schoolhouse, standing on the left and a little back from the road. It was one story and lights showed in the windows. Vehicles were parked haphazardly in front.

"Stay with the jeep," Boone said to the other two.

He went up a few steps and across a narrow porch and entered a hallway. The room on the right was crowded with noisy men. The door to the room on the left was closed. A major, uniform muddy and torn, squeezed out of the press and rapped on the closed door. Boone grabbed his shoulder and turned him around.

"Where's Colonel Brazos?" he demanded.

For a moment the major gaped stupidly at the star on Boone's helmet as more men crowded the door to peer out into the hall. Then his hand dropped to the .45 at his hip and Miles saw hysteria creep into his eyes.

"Who wants to know?" he asked thickly.

"I want to know! I'm General Boone!"

"Oh, no you don't," the major yelled, his voice cracking a little. "You don't pull that! You're that phony general the German lieutenant told us about! Grab him, men!"

Four

FOR A MOMENT Miles Boone stood blinking in the light which flowed into the hallway of the schoolhouse from the open door at his right. Once or twice before in his life he'd seen what panic could do to men; it was like an epidemic from which even good men were not immune if conditions were right. Its presence here was evident in this major's wild eyes — in the distorted faces of the men who crowded the doorway behind him.

"All right," Boone said sharply. "What's the trouble here? I'm General Boone and I'm bringing an armored combat command into Rigny. Who's in command here . . ."

He was reaching for his identification when the major's gun came free from its holster and was pointed at his belly. "Get your hands on top your head," the major barked. "Willis, search him — his identification will be forged, like that lieutenant's was. But we'll have a look at it and . . ."

He stopped as feet scraped roughly against the boards of the porch outside. Lute Heard came in, his seamed face working violently as he squirmed and spat like a cat at the two burly M.P.s who held him by the arms and hustled him along, his feet off the floor most of the time. Behind them came two more men with Corporal Millikin, the radio operator, held between them. Millikin's eyes were scared and his mouth was a thin line.

"These two birds were settin' in the jeep, Major," one of the M.P.s said. "They're Germans, all right. I asked this old goat who is Popeye the Sailor's girl friend and he cussed me out and said he'd as soon associate with an M.P. as a sailor."

"I'll old-goat you, you goon!" Lute yelled, his voice hoarse with fury. "Get your paws off me before I bend you into a pretzel — I was soldierin' in this man's Army when you were wearin' three-cornered pants, blast you!"

"You'll bend nobody," the M.P. began.

"Hold it!" Boone said sharply.

He recalled the odd countersigns they'd been asked by the tank destroyer sergeant as they'd come into town — everyday things familiar to most Americans but which Germans, masquerading in American uniforms, wouldn't be likely to know. A crude but effective security measure that had been improvised to meet the threat of forged conventional credentials.

"I believe Olive Oyl is Popeye's girl friend, Major," he said, his lips quirking briefly as the macabre humor of this situation struck him. "Sergeant Heard has been so busy soldiering for the past twenty-five years that he hasn't had time to keep up with the funny papers. Now suppose we cut out this clowning. Who is in command here? Where is he?"

The major hesitated, scowling as he looked at the brigadier general's star on Boone's helmet. This guy don't look like a German, he was thinking. And if he's not, I better not get my neck in no higher sling than it is already. Indecision showed in his face for a moment; then the muzzle of the .45 slowly drooped. The major clicked the safety back on and reluctantly returned the weapon to its holster. He mopped sweat from his forehead.

"I'm sorry, General," he said thickly. "Everything is all messed up and I guess we're pretty jumpy around here. We caught a German, dressed up like an American lieutenant, a couple of hours ago. He came in with phony orders . . ."

"What kind of orders?"

"He said the regiment was to withdraw from its positions and retire across the Vaar at once. We spotted him as a phony when one of our people heard his driver speaking German over the jeep radio. We grabbed them both."

"Good," Miles said. "Where are they?"

This was the first break he'd had today, he was thinking. The chances were that a German officer, caught in an American uniform behind American lines, would talk, knowing that his life was forfeit if he didn't. Maybe what he had to tell would give Boone some inkling as to what really was going on.

The major — his name was Walker — scrubbed a hand over his red face as he looked back at Miles Boone in the uncertain light that filled the hallway. He was beginning to snap out of it a little. The presence of a general here was reassuring.

"Dead, sir," he said. "Colonel Brazos ordered that both of them be shot."

"Did you find out anything from them first?" Boone demanded, his voice rasping. "Anything at all?"

"We found out they were Germans dressed in American uniforms," Walker said stubbornly. "That was enough."

"And shot away your chance to find out what's going on," Boone snapped. He looked impatiently at the faces that still filled the doorway to the lighted room — at the M.P.s who still waited in the hall. "Haven't these men got anything to do? If they haven't, you'd better send them up front where they can be of some use."

He noted with sour amusement that the faces in the doorway magically disappeared and that the scrape of the M.P.s' boots were hasty on the porch. "Go back and tell Dunn to get up here with the scout car," he said to Lute. "Have him leave a man at the edge of town to guide CCB in case it gets here before we get back. That's not likely."

"Where we going?" Lute asked, still sulking over the treatment he had received. "If it ain't too much to ask."

"Up front to have a look for ourselves," Boone said. "After I've found out what the situation is here."

"I hope we take them M.P.s with us," Lute said,

stamping angrily toward the door. "I'd like to personally give them a little taste of war."

"All right," Boone said curtly to Walker. "Where's Colonel Brazos? Up front? When do you expect him back?"

"No, sir, he's not up front," Walker said and jerked his head towards the closed door. "He's in there. The door's locked and he won't come out, General."

For an instant Boone looked back at the major with unbelieving eyes. "What do you mean — he won't come out?" he asked sharply then. "Is he wounded?"

"No, sir," Walker answered in a flat tone. "He's not wounded. I think he's gone nuts, sir."

Miles Boone tried the door — it was locked as Walker had said. "Break it in," he said to the major and they put their weight against the door and the flimsy lock gave way. There was no light in the room but Boone could see a man's head and shoulders silhouetted against a window.

"Bring a light," he said to Walker.

The major came back shortly, holding a Coleman lantern shoulder high. A man sat at a child's desk, his hands flat in front of him and his eyes staring straight ahead. His face was thin and pinched and the pupils of his eyes were contracted, Boone saw as he moved around in front of him.

Boone turned abruptly away. "Come on," he said to Walker. "Better keep someone with him until he can be evacuated — heaven only knows when that will be. You're the executive?"

"Yes, sir."

"Fill me in on the situation as you know it. I'll find out the rest of it for myself up front."

The watch on his wrist indicated that it was a little after 1900 — seven o'clock — as Major General Clark Blocker sat behind a desk in his command post at Couteaux and sipped thoughtfully at coffee that had grown cold while he was talking with Corps on the phone. The window on his left was black with night but he knew that beyond it snow was falling. Nasty weather for operations — but then you could seldom choose the weather in which you fought. Things had certainly come unstuck all of a sudden, he was thinking grimly. Somewhere somebody had goofed.

He'd gotten little information from Corps. Nobody yet had any clear idea as to just what had happened this morning but it was apparent that massive German attacks, heavy in armor, had hit the front all the way from Monschau in the north to Echternach, some eighty-five miles south of there. It was rumored that the better part of an American division was cut off on the Schnee Eifel; still another division was being overrun east of Wiltz.

There were a million other rumors.

German parachutists had seized the crossings of the Vaar and the Ourthe rivers; parachutists had been dropped in the outskirts of Liège and Spa.

Storm troopers, wearing stolen G.I. uniforms and riding in stolen American jeeps, had infiltrated the lines and were spreading confusion and panic. SS Lieutenant Colonel Otto Skorzeny — the same fellow who had kidnapped Mussolini from Marshal Badoglio — was in Paris with a group of picked men. His mission: kidnap or kill the Supreme Commander and key members of his staff. Who knew who was friend and who was foe?

A million rumors.

"Rot!" Blocker had said into the phone. He was a man who didn't scare easily and he was accustomed to speak his mind. "You birds back there have got the wind up and are acting like a bunch of old women! What's the situation at Rigny?"

The staff officer at the other end of the line hadn't known what the situation at Rigny was. A Colonel Brazos, commanding an infantry regiment, had established his command post there, but his division commander hadn't been in communication with him since noon. In view of the rumor that parachutists had seized the bridges over the Vaar, perhaps it would be better if Hammerhead Division moved south along the river towards Bastogne, instead. By tomorrow maybe the situation would have cleared a little.

Blocker had snorted into the phone. "Are those orders?" he had demanded. "If they are, I want them from the Old Man himself! He said Hammerhead was to go to Rigny. Until he personally tells me differently, to Rigny it goes! And confound your rumors!"

The officer at the other end of the line had hemmed and hawed and said that the Old Man wasn't there — he'd been called back for a conference at Army headquarters . . . no telling when he would return. So Major General Clark Blocker had hung up on him and now he sat and sipped at the cold coffee and studied the big map on the wall in front of him with his dark, big-nosed face thoughtful and his eyes narrowed. The glare of the Coleman lantern brought the map's details out with a stark clarity.

Miles Boone would have turned Combat Command B east at Saint Heye, he guessed. He would have crossed the Vaar at Vaaracre; that was the way Blocker himself would have done it if he'd been commanding CCB, and he credited Boone with having no less military savvy than he had. He'd had no word from Boone since the 1400 report that Combat Command B was on the road. Therefore the chances were good that Boone had run into no serious trouble so far. That meant that he could be in Rigny by now.

As for those rumors about parachutists seizing the Vaar crossings — nuts, they were pure rumor! You could hear anything in war, especially in a situation as fouled up as this one was. In spite of this reassurance a faint crease showed across Blocker's forehead as he stared at the map. The tiny worry which had been gnawing at the back of his mind for the past hour began to gnaw harder now.

Suppose — one chance in a thousand — that

those rumors were true and the Germans *had* captured the crossings over the Vaar? In that case Combat Command B would be cut off at Rigny with an unfordable river at its back. It would be in a spot where no help could get to it. So, with heaven knew how many panzer divisions in front of it, CCB was a dead duck. He could kiss one good combat command good-bye.

Blocker got out of his chair without haste and walked to the door. "Ed," he said to his chief of staff, "get Lovell and Ferguson in here. I want to hear from them why a Pentagon general, who has been here just two days, can get his combat command on the road in two hours when it takes them until midnight to do it. Get them here on the double, Ed!"

General Melvin Lovell had Combat Command A; Colonel George Ferguson, Combat Command Reserve. When they came hurriedly out of Major General Blocker's office a little later, both of them looked badly shaken. Colonel Ed Watson, the chief of staff, shuffled papers and kept his eyes discreetly on his desk as they went by. He knew when he was well off.

The conference in Clark Blocker's office paid off because the rest of the Hammerhead Division, Armored, turned south on the Liège-Bastogne road a good two hours before midnight. General Blocker rode with the column; as he sat in the command car, peering out at the falling snow, a number of thoughts were running through his mind. They concerned Miles Boone. Clark Blocker did not communicate them to his aide, Lieutenant Pudge Dreyfuss, who rode on the leather seat beside him.

He moved fast enough getting CCB on the road, Blocker was thinking grudgingly. And there was nothing wrong about the way he went after those replacement tanks — Nash needed to have a fire built under him, anyway. But will he fight? I've got a hunch that what we've seen before is peanuts to what we're sticking our noses into now. Benny Martell, I wish it was you up ahead of us tonight because it's going to be bad. Pretty bad.

At Saint Heye crossroads Ed Smith, commanding the armored reconnaissance battalion, waited for Clark Blocker. The bridge over the Vaar at Vaaracre had been blown up, Ed told Blocker soberly. Either by German saboteurs or retreating Americans. The next bridge was some twenty miles south. Likely it was blown, too.

"We'll go find out," Blocker said grimly. "This is going to be worse than I thought it would be."

He was soon going to find out whether or not Miles Boone would fight, he was thinking glumly as the column began to move again. Because Combat Command B was going to be on its own for the better part of the next twenty-four hours. Maybe longer than that, the way things were developing.

Combat Command B inched along the Rigny road like cold clabber trying to flow uphill. Darkness had fallen three hours before, and the town was still ten miles distant. Straggler vehicles inched along the opposite side of the road in a tangled stream. Traffic jams formed that took valuable minutes to unravel. Butch Marcus, in the lead tank, could no longer, in his own words, "run right over the crummy buzzards," because there were just too many of them.

The tank column had ground to another of its infuriating halts when Summer, the executive, came back to where Colonel Nash sat impatiently in his jeep. Nash did not feel that directing traffic befitted the dignity of the acting commander of CCB. He'd been studying his map in the dull glow of a flashlight; now he looked up, his handsome face petulant in the reflected light.

"Well, what is it this time?" he demanded. "What's holding us up now?"

"It's just no good, Colonel," Summer said, mopping melting snow from his face. "The road ahead is jammed from shoulder to shoulder with stuff and there's more trying to get in from a side road. I never saw such a . . ."

"Order the drivers to get out of the way," Nash snapped. "You're an officer, aren't you?"

"Colonel, those guys aren't taking orders any more. Not from me or anybody else."

"We'll see about that," Nash said through his teeth. He stepped down into the slushy underfooting. "Come on."

He stalked ahead into the darkness, his back straight and his shoulders squared — as they had been when he'd marched by in review in front of

his company at West Point. After all, he was thinking, Major Summer was nothing really but a civil-
ian in uniform. He didn't know how to handle soldiers.

A big truck had skidded halfway across the road,
its front bumper hooked into the fender of an
ambulance. Behind, other vehicles were piled up.
Jeeps, vans, pickups, four-by-fours. Men shouted
and cursed; engines backfired. Nash stalked to the
truck and yanked the cab door open.

"Back this truck into the ditch," he ordered
crisply. "Haven't you got sense enough to . . ."

A rough voice snarled at him. "Get your puss
out of my cab," it said. "I back this bus no
place, buster! I'm gettin' out of here and you're
not stopping me!"

Shock showed on Nash's good-looking face in
the glow of the headlights. No one had ever spoken
like that to him before — certainly no enlisted
man. His voice rose, thin with rage. Other men
crowded up now to listen.

"I'm Colonel Nash of Combat Command B!" he
yelled. "I order you to . . ."

The truck driver's rough voice cut him off again,
meaner than before. "I don't care if you're Lady
Godiva on a horse," it said. "You ain't giving me
no orders!"

Pudgy Captain Jeremiah Potts, crouched on the
hull of Butch Marcus' Sherman tank a few yards
down the road, could hear what was going on. So
could Butch, standing in the turret of the tank.
Nash's voice was lifting again.

"Get this man's name and organization, Major Summer!" he was saying. "We'll see whether or not . . ."

"Sergeant," Potts said softly, "we don't seem to be getting anywhere, do we? I'm afraid taking names and organizations isn't going to have much effect on that mob back there right at the moment."

"A tank gun'd do better," Butch said sourly.

"Exactly the thing I was thinking, Sergeant," Potts said. "Fire the first one a little high — we don't want to hurt anybody. Not yet, anyway."

Butch Marcus needed no second word. He spoke a curt command and the breech of the Sherman's 75-mm cannon snicked shut as the round slammed home. The muzzle of the gun lifted — flamed orange as the concussion clapped at the ears of Butch Marcus and Jerry Potts. The yelling in front suddenly stopped and the night was quiet except for the grind of engines. Then Potts' voice, drawling but wicked, carried in the darkness.

"I recommend you get that junk out of the road," it said. "The next shot could go right into the middle of it — this is Combat Command B and we're going to Rigny."

The big truck backed into the ditch; the ambulance went across the road into the other ditch. The road began to clear. Butch bent to yell at his driver.

"Crank her up, Pole!"

Captain Potts was aware of an angry face peering up at him through the gloom. Nash's voice, hoarse with anger, reached him above the racket of the tank's engine.

"What do you mean by firing on our own troops, Potts?" it asked. "Consider yourself under arrest! Do you understand?"

"Yes, sir," Potts said.

"Well, anyhow, we're rollin' again," Butch said from the turret as the tank treads began to clank. "That's something — I wouldn't worry too much about being under arrest, Captain. If that general had of been here I bet he'd of done just what you did."

The command post of the second battalion of the infantry regiment was in a farmhouse that had been well shot up. The battalion commander, a lean and hard-bitten man named McCrumm, pointed to a map in the flickering light of a candle and explained the disposition of his battalion to Miles Boone. His three rifle companies were dug in here along a ridge, he said. Not a bad position. The flanks were pretty well anchored and his heavy weapons company had the front and flanks covered with supporting fire. For awhile today it had been a bit rough, but now he figured that they had things pretty well in hand for the moment. Miles liked the way he talked.

"What happened this morning?" he asked.

"They jumped us out of the fog," McCrumm said. "We were all spread out, you see. Had to be, considering the amount of front we had to cover. Only way we could do it was with strong points

— pretty far apart — up in front with support groups covering the gaps. Lucky in the end that we had it that way because it helped us to gather ourselves together later on. Not that we didn't get a good bloody nose in the process."

"How do you stand on casualties?"

"About 15 per cent. That's not too bad considering that the Germans hit us hard with tanks around noon. Big buzzards — Tigers. We had quite a time of it for awhile."

"Who's the senior battalion commander in the regiment?" Boone asked. McCrumm looked at him with mild astonishment, then shrugged in the candlelight. A German shell burst on the ridge two hundred yards in front of the farmhouse and its concussion rattled the windows.

"One-fifty stuff," McCrumm said absently. "I ain't heard any of ours all day — it'd be a welcome sound. I guess Charley Pelt is senior, General, if he's still alive. I'm next."

Boone made up his mind swiftly. "Who's your executive?" he asked as Lute Heard came in, stamping the snow from his feet as he stood waiting.

"Joe Rafferty," McCrumm said.

"A good man?"

"The best."

"Put him in command of the battalion. I'm taking you back to Rigny with me, Colonel. You're commanding the regiment as of now. Tell Rafferty to hold here at all costs. I'll send him tank support as soon as CCB comes up."

McCrumm looked up quickly, his sharp features seeming more thinly drawn in the flickering candlelight. "You mean that Colonel Brazos has bought it, sir?"

"Colonel Brazos was staring into space when I saw him last," Miles said grimly and saw the shock that ran across McCrumm's face. "On the way back to Rigny I'll give you the situation as I know it. Get hold of Rafferty. We haven't got much time."

"Yes, sir," McCrumm said.

"I got through to CCB on the radio," Lute said, his voice sour. "As far as I can make out, they're still about eight miles from Rigny, gallopin' like a snail with the road all junked up with straggler traffic. Nash's got Potts under arrest."

"Under arrest for what?"

"Shootin' off a tank gun. Potts figured the best way to get through was to shoot his way through. Nash about had pups."

"I'll give Potts a medal," Boone said through his teeth and added bitingly descriptive words concerning Nelson Nash. "Get the jeep cranked up — we're heading back there."

Lute squinted and grinned his leathery grin in the candlelight. "I feel better," he said. "I ain't heard some of those words since we used to soldier together in the Armored Brigade. I was afraid you were goin' soft, Miles."

They jolted back over the road toward Rigny, McCrumm hunched in back beside Corporal Millikin as Boone talked to him over his shoulder. The snow still fell. Lute had the headlights on to make better time, disregarding the fact that German patrols might be on the prowl. The twin beams bored into the falling snowflakes that drifted down like dead white bugs.

Boone was reviewing the map of the surrounding country in his mind as he had seen it back at the schoolhouse. Three main roads intersected at Rigny. One coming from Maastricht to the northeast; one coming from Eifel to the south. The main road was the one that they were on; it ran east and west from the Our and it would be the one down which the main German effort would come, he guessed. He spoke of that to McCrumm.

They'd build up the position the second battalion held astride the east-west road. As the other two battalions could be gathered together they'd set up similar blocking positions on the Maastricht and Eifel roads. Tanks would be used sparingly to reinforce the infantry; the main part of Combat Command B would be held in Rigny as a mobile striking force at any part of the semi-perimeter that was threatened.

"Sounds good," McCrumm said.

"If Combat Command B ever gets to Rigny," Lute mumbled under his breath.

They came back into Rigny again. Boone, glancing at his wrist watch, was dismayed to see that it was less than a half hour before midnight. In the schoolhouse Major Walker was waiting for them, his red face agitated.

"There's somebody called Stampede One calling

for you over the radio, sir," he said to Boone. "They seem to want you pretty bad."

Stampede One was the code name for Major General Clark Blocker, Miles thought wryly. He thought also how little he actually knew of the situation up front and of Combat Command B still stalled somewhere back along the road. He was quite sure that his conversation with Clark Blocker wasn't going to be cordial.

The message center was in a house across the street and he headed for it, Lute at his heels. There was one source of satisfaction to him in all of this mess, though; Lieutenant Colonel Mike McCrumm had landed in that confusion in the schoolhouse like a bursting shell. He had a good man in Mc-Crumm, Boone knew.

The radio operator fiddled with his dials and spoke into the mike. "Dusty calling Stampede One . . . Dusty calling Stampede One . . . come in, Stampede One . . ."

Presently he said, "Okay, General," and held out the mike. Boone took it and pressed the button.

"Stetson One," he said, giving his own code name. "Over."

The receiver squawked tinnily with a confused jumble for a moment; then General Blocker's voice came through, distorted but recognizable. He didn't bother with code.

"What's the situation there?" he asked.

Boone told him, speaking carefully and using double talk that he knew the other would understand. Combat Command B was still somewhere between Vaaracre and Rigny; the situation up front was confused. As of now, things were not critical.

"As of tomorrow morning things are likely to be good and critical," Blocker said harshly. "I sent you up there to command CCB — not to go wandering over half of Belgium where I can't get hold of you when I want you! Get back to your command! Move it to where it's supposed to be! Understand?"

"I understand," Boone said tightly.

"It's going to be late tomorrow before you get any help. Maybe even later than that. But I want that place held! So, by heaven, you hold it until I get there! Do you understand that?"

"I understand that."

"That's good." Boone got the sarcasm despite the tinniness of the receiver. "Because I want to tell you something. You're getting mighty close to that first slip."

"Yes, sir."

"That's all. Out!"

Boone handed the mike back to the operator and turned into the snowy night again. The gnawing in his belly reminded him that he hadn't eaten since morning and tiredness, born of scant sleep during the past three days, was an ache in his shoulders. Lute Heard fell into step beside him as they went back to the schoolhouse across the way.

"You ever think that maybe you could've been a doctor?" Lute asked. "Or maybe a lawyer — or even pumped gas into jalopies at a filling station? It'd beat this."

"I guess it would," Miles said absently.

For some reason he was suddenly thinking of Janet de Ceilly as he'd first seen her in the farmhouse kitchen the night that he'd come to Combat Command B. There had been such a poised pride about her as she had stood there looking at him in the light of the Coleman lantern. Yet, beneath that poise, he had sensed a warmth that had come through such a little while later. It would be nice to be back. . . .

He put the thought angrily out of his mind as he climbed the schoolhouse steps. McCrumm was speaking into a telephone in clipped, hard tones and Boone waited until he was finished. Then the lieutenant colonel put the phone down and stood up.

"I want every man and every vehicle that you can spare from your headquarters company, McCrumm," Boone said curtly. "The men will be armed. We're going to clear out the traffic jam on the Vaaracre road from this end — and I'll be sending you a bunch of recruits. Put them to work."

"I'll do just that, General," McCrumm grunted. "I've got telephone communication again with the second battalion. They need replacements up there. I can use all you can send."

They moved out ten minutes later. At the far side of town they picked up Lieutenant Helvar Dunn and his scout car — Boone had sent him word earlier to stay with the tank-destroyer sergeant and

see that no more traffic left Rigny to clog the
Vaaracre road. That should help some, he was
thinking; for the first part of the way, at least, the
road should be clear.

To the sergeant he said, "As before, nobody still
leaves Rigny, Sergeant. Pretty soon we'll be sending people back here. Let them in but don't let
them out again. Got it?"

"You bet I got it," the sergeant said. "It's goin' to
be a downright pleasure, General."

It took them twenty minutes to catch up to the
tail of the straggler column. Men poured out of
the little convoy of trucks that had come from
Rigny. Men angry with themselves for the panic
that had gripped them earlier; men smarting with
the knowledge that they had demeaned themselves
in the eyes of this slender general in the muddy
uniform who now led them. They vented their
wrath on those who had behaved worse than they,
the ones who had run.

A T/5 headquarters clerk, weighing about as
much as a Girl Scout wringing wet, yanked open
the door of a stalled two-and-a-half ton truck and
jabbed the muzzle of a carbine at the four men
crammed into the cab. The smallest of them out-
weighed the T/5 by forty pounds. There were mut-
ters from within.

"Get this bucket turned around!" the T/5
snarled. "You guys are going up front for the first
time in your lives! You're going to fight!"

"Who says?" an angry voice asked.

"I said!" the T/5 snapped.

They got the truck turned around. Other men were herded into it. Presently it pulled back along the road to Rigny, the T/5 riding it cockily, his carbine held on his hip.

Obstructing vehicles were butted off into the ditch; others were loaded with stray G.I.s and dispatched to Rigny. Little by little order began to come out of the chaos on the Vaaracre road. It was three o'clock in the morning when Miles Boone got back to Combat Command B. He found Nelson Nash arguing with an ordnance colonel over the right of way at a side road.

Major General Blocker sat in the command post of an infantry division at a little town called Troisvierges on the east bank of the Vaar. There was a bridge here but it wasn't big enough to bear the weight of the thirty-five-ton Sherman tanks, so the Hammerhead Division was continuing to move south towards the bridge at Brey. Blocker had just finished talking with Miles Boone and he felt tired and old and he wondered when this would all be over.

The door opened and another man, gaunt and worried-looking and also wearing two stars, came into the room. He sat down with a faint sigh and began to fill a pipe from a worn tobacco pouch as he looked across the table at Blocker.

"Get your man, Clark?" he asked.

"I got him," Blocker said heavily. "He'd been running around with the fool infantry somewhere while his combat command's stuck back along the road."

"It's the fool infantry that's up where the bloody noses are being dished out," the second general said with a little asperity. "You tankers think you're the only ones in this war."

Blocker stirred his big frame in his chair. "Sorry, Steve," he said. "I guess we're not much help right now — running around headless while we try to get across a river. Well, thanks for your help. I'd better get moving."

"I've got coffee coming," the infantry general said. "You can spare a little more time. When you come right down to it, Clark, generals aren't an awful lot of use in my book once the fighting starts. It's the poor guy up in the front line foxhole or riding the assault tank wave that wins."

Blocker's heavy, hook-nosed face looked darkly sardonic in the lamplight. "A few more remarks like that and we'll read you out of the club, Steve," he said. "But, just between you and me, I couldn't agree with you more. Maybe that's why I teed off on Boone the way I did a little while ago."

"Rough on him, eh?"

"Like a cob. He's racing around up there at Rigny doing a captain's job while he should be back commanding CCB. That's what he's paid for! Even at that he's doing something useful. Maybe that's the thing that rides me—I feel pretty useless back here right now, Steve."

An orderly brought coffee, black and steaming, in canteen cups; he put the cups on the table and went out again. Blocker lighted a cigarette and the two men sat in silence for a moment, sipping gingerly across metal hot enough to sear their lips.

"Rigny," the infantry general said finally. "That's in Colby's sector," and he named the division to the north.

Blocker nodded absently. "When Miles Boone joined the division, I told him if he made one slip I'd break him," he said. "When I said it, I didn't know that I'd be dumping the weight of a corps on his shoulders. Rigny is the key to the whole Ardennes. Either Rigny is held until we get some of the pieces swept together or the Germans will have a clear shot at the Vaar—after that the Ourthe, maybe the Meuse."

"I agree," the infantry general said. "My division boundary runs a dozen miles south of there. I haven't been too happy knowing that the security of my north flank depends on how well Brazos defends Rigny. I guess maybe I feel better knowing that your man is there, Clark."

Blocker looked at the other sardonically along his big nose. "So far, Boone has sat out this war on the seat of his pants in the Pentagon."

The worried look deepened in the other's thin face. "I didn't know that," he said. "His first fight? How long before you'll be able to back him up, do you think?"

Blocker moodily put his canteen cup on the table and got out of his chair to study the map tacked on the wall. The bridge being knocked out at Vaaracre was a bad break; it was a long way south to the bridge at Brey and, once across there, if they got across, the road net involved a long swing to the east before they could turn north towards Rigny again. He scaled the distances with his eye while he calculated the rate at which the Hammerhead Division could move on congested roads.

"With luck, the head of the division might start arriving there about dark tomorrow, Steve. That's the best I can hope for. It could be a lot longer."

The infantry general absently scratched a match on the seat of his trousers and looked at it without holding it to his dead pipe; the flame burned down to scorch his fingers and he dropped the match to the floor, still with that abstract look on his face. Blocker moved back to the table and picked up his helmet with the two stars. He put it on, chin strap dangling.

"I've known you for a long while, Clark," the other general said finally. "You're a Simon Legree when it comes to driving men and you're ruthless with weak commanders. It's made you a good division commander and the Hammerhead a great division. If you had doubts about Boone why did you take him, and if you still have doubts why don't you let someone else bring the division on while you cut across to Rigny and take over things there yourself?"

Blocker drank the last of his coffee. "Just one thing stops me, Steve," he said. "A thing that happened at West Point."

"So?"

"A long time ago," Blocker went on. "Boone was

a plebe and I was a first classman. We had a grudge fight and I beat the tar out of him. He came back for more and each time I beat him again. The guy just didn't know when he was licked. Well, maybe he still doesn't know. Maybe I'm going to need that kind."

"They're not easy to find."

"I know. Boone just may be one."

The command post of Combat Command B was established in a house on the eastern outskirts of Rigny just as a dirty gray was beginning to lighten the eastern sky. Again the snow had turned to a drizzling rain which soaked men to the skin while the cold wind cut through to the marrow of their bones. The morning of December 17 in Belgium. Not a nice morning.

Miles Boone, red-eyed from lack of sleep and weary from labors of the last thirty hours, sat in a plainly furnished room that looked out on the east-west road while he sipped coffee. He had sent tanks, armored infantry, and engineers to reinforce Rafferty's infantry battalion on the ridge. Armored patrols were probing to the south and the northeast in the direction of Eifel and Maastricht. So far they had reported no contact.

For the moment there was nothing to do but wait, Boone was thinking as the coffee warmed him. Nothing to do about the Germans, that was. But a chore that he didn't relish remained to be done here in Combat Command B.

Lute Heard came through the door. "I sent for

Nash like you asked," he said. "What you goin' to do about him, Miles?"

Boone didn't answer at once. Earlier in the morning, when he'd gotten back to CCB and found the column stalled while Nash argued the right of way with an ordnance colonel, he'd been too furious to trust himself to speak. He'd curtly ordered Nash back to the armored regiment and the latter had gone sullenly. Now he was faced with two choices and he didn't like either of them.

He could relieve Nash and send him to the rear. If he did that what assurance did he have that Nash's successor would be any better? Miles knew none of the other officers in the armored regiment; time had been too short for him to assess their value. Or he could really chew Nash out this time and offer him another chance. That meant he ran the risk of having Nash let him down again. Neither solution was attractive.

"I don't know," he said finally to Lute. "Play it by ear, I guess. Nash is a professional — a good soldier if he'd only learn to throw away the book now and then."

Heard's face got sharper in the growing light. "I'd tie a can on him, Miles," he said waspishly. "That guy'll cut your throat one of these days if you don't."

"I'll see," Miles said tiredly.

Lute went out, closing the door behind him. A few minutes later a rap came at the door. Nash, Boone thought. I may as well get it over with.

It wasn't Nash. It was Captain Leroy Jefferson,

the S-3, with a message from Potts who had gone
with the patrol that was probing towards Maastricht. It had come over the radio "in the clear,"
uncoded, and it wasn't reassuring.

GERMAN ARMORED COLUMN OBSERVED ADVANCING
SOUTHWEST TOWARDS RIGNY ON MAASTRICHT
ROAD ESTIMATE IT AT REGIMENTAL STRENGTH
WITH TRUCKED INFANTRY FOLLOWING. NOTHING
BEHIND US ON RIGNY ROAD EXCEPT PARTS INFANTRY
BATTALION BADLY DISORGANIZED. — POTTS

"It looks like trouble," Boone said quietly.
"Yes, sir," Leroy agreed, his long face mournful.
An orderly came to the door. "Colonel Nash is
here, General," he said.

Five

COLONEL NELSON NASH made his way through the drizzle toward CCB's command post in the gray, unhappy light of the coming dawn. His handsome face was sulky but there was a faint apprehension in his eyes. He'd been expecting the summons ever since Miles Boone had sent him back to the armored regiment at three o'clock this morning on the Vaaracre road.

Nash hadn't been just apprehensive then as the general's slight figure, muddy from head to foot, had appeared out of the darkness. In the dim glow of the headlights he'd seen the fury in Boone's eyes; he'd heard the rasp in Boone's voice as the latter had relieved young Potts from arrest and sent him back to duty. He'd expected that Boone would turn on him then, blasting him with invective and relieving him on the spot.

Boone hadn't.

"Get back to your regiment, Nash," was all that he had said. "I'll take over here."

For a moment Nash had felt an almost overwhelming surge of relief as he'd gone back along the column. As the night wore away, though, the relief wore away with it. Now the apprehension

114

had come back a dozenfold. What was Boone planning to do to him? Nausea gripped his stomach as he went through the rain. Boone could ruin him professionally, he knew. Maybe Boone had spent the war in the Pentagon, but a general's word still carried weight.

He'd beat Boone to the punch, he decided. He'd ask to be relieved before the other had a chance to light into him. Then he knew, sickly, that that wouldn't do. Combat Command B was on the edge of a fight — perhaps the worst fight it had ever had. And an officer who asked to be relieved on the verge of battle was dead as far as the Army was concerned.

He started for the steps of the house where the command post lay and saw Leroy Jefferson leaving the place at a run. Nash was too busy with his own thoughts to wonder why. He entered the house, asked a sergeant where General Boone was, and went in the direction the sergeant pointed. He rapped at the door.

"Come in," Boone's voice said.

The general had his helmet on his head, strap hanging, as he bent over a map on the desk. The mud had dried a little on his clothes but smears of it were still on his stubbled face. Nash halted and turned out his salute.

"Nash reporting as ordered, sir."

"Uh, yes," Boone said, not looking up. "Just a minute, Colonel." He scaled a distance on the map.

Nash stayed at rigid attention, feeling uncomfortably warm in spite of the chilliness of the room.

He'd forgotten all of the things he'd meant to say. All he wished was that Boone would get this over with.

Boone tossed his dividers down on the map and straightened. "I'm splitting Combat Command B into two task forces," he said brusquely. "The first, Task Force Prebble, will accompany me." Rapidly he named the elements of the force. A battalion of tanks, supporting armored infantry and field artillery and tank destroyers and engineers. Lieutenant Colonel Prebble, leading the tank battalion, would be in command. "The second task force will consist of the remainder of CCB less those elements already out on specific missions. You will command it."

Boone's voice was impersonal. Nash, expecting a vastly different reception, relaxed from his stiff attention, his face showing conflicting emotions.

"Yes, sir," he said. "What . . ."

"Task Force Nash will remain here in Rigny in reserve for the moment," Miles went on, as if brushing Nash's words aside. "You will be prepared to move to the front on any of the three roads running out of here depending on how the situation develops. I will accompany Task Force Prebble to block an armored threat reported on the Maastricht road. Any questions?"

"No, sir."

"Then that's all. Maintain liaison with McCrumm commanding the infantry. He's a good man. I'll keep in touch with you by radio. Let me know at once if anything develops to the south."

"Yes, sir," Nash said again. He knew that he shouldn't push his luck; that he should quit while he was still ahead. But he had to ask the question. "What about last night, sir?"

"Last night?"

Nash felt the red creeping up into his face. Confound it, he had looked pretty bad, standing there beating his gums with that ordnance colonel when Miles Boone had come upon him. He had at least a chewing out coming to him.

"Uh," he said lamely. "I mean when you rejoined us on the Vaaracre road, General."

For a moment Boone looked thoughtfully at the other with chill gray eyes that told nothing. "Oh, that," he said finally. "I haven't had time to make up my mind about it, Nash."

As Nelson Nash left the command post he didn't know whether he should feel relieved or in a worse state of uncertainty than he'd been in before. One thing Boone's hard eyes had told him — the incident had not been forgotten. Not by a long sight.

The road, coming from Maastricht, wound down a snowy slope and crossed a bridge over a little stream, then began to climb another slope towards a V in a low ridge crowned with firs. The five medium tanks of the tank platoon were drawn off on either side of the V and concealed by the trees. Butch Marcus' big Sherman was the nearest to the road. Just back of the brow of the ridge, on the Rigny side, was the scout car in which Captain Potts had been riding. It had rejoined the platoon a quarter hour ago, bringing news of German armor on the Maastricht road.

Butch leaned against the edge of the turret and rubbed at his bristled cheeks with a grimy hand, rearranging the grease marks there into a clownish pattern. He glanced down the road to where Jeremiah Potts, looking amiable and pudgy in a field jacket that was too small for him, talked with Lieutenant Angsberg, the tank platoon commander.

"You know," Butch said to Steve Reilly, who was sitting on the tank's hull, "so help me, I'm gettin' to be right fond of the Fat Boy. He kind of grows on me. Take last night when he was all set to shoot them guys out of the road."

Reilly spat critically into the snow. "If he grows any more, he's going to bust right out of that field jacket," he grunted. "What you doing, Butch? Bucking for another stripe? First you say almost nice things about a general. Now you're doing the same for a captain. The general part was the worst — you never had no use for generals before. It bugs me."

"You got to be charitable," Butch said placidly, scratching himself. "The way that I figure is that even if a guy does wear stars on his shoulder he can't be all bad." He turned his head again to look at Potts and Angsberg. "What you think them two are cookin' up down there?"

"Nothing we're going to like," Reilly said. "Personally, I'd just as soon drag out of here. I never did like to fight in winter anyway."

"Who said anything about fightin'? We come here for a picnic. Ain't you heard?"

Pole, the driver, suddenly poked his head through the hatch. "Somebody say picnic?" he asked. "That I could go for! Pass the fried chicken, Maw."

"Get back under your rock," Reilly growled. "Drivers are supposed to be seen and not heard, dumpfkopf."

"Nuts to you," Pole said.

Across the way in Sergeant Shultz's No. 3 tank, Shultz argued with Corporal Tinker, his driver. Tinker came from Coosky, South Carolina; he had a wife and four kids back there and was an elder in the church, when he was at home. He had no business being in the Army but was here because he thought it was his duty to be. He and Sergeant Shultz engaged in long arguments about religion and marriage and the Democratic party.

"Maybe marriage is all right for guys like you," Shultz was saying. "You're the steady, vegitatin' type, Tink. Go to church and pass the plate on Sunday and all that. All I was saying is that it just ain't for guys like me."

"Marriage is for everybody," Tinker said.

He was a long, lathy man with a solemn face and tow hair that seeped from beneath his driver's helmet. He had a slow way of speaking as though he was chewing each word. In the evenings he read from the small Testament he carried. At times some of the rest of the platoon would ask him to read aloud and he was glad to do so. They didn't ask often, though.

"Uh-uh," Shultz disagreed. He was small and wiry and tough. "You're wrong there, Tink. I know it ain't for me — I tried it once. The fights that me and my old lady had were worse than the battle of Gettysburg."

"You've got to give and take, Sergeant," Tinker said. "That's what makes a marriage really work."

"We give and took all right," Shultz said reflectively. "I give her my pay and she took off with a slick cigar peddler from Detroit. I never even tried to get her back."

"You should have. It was your duty."

"Naw, I knew when I was well off," Shultz said. "She was a welter and I never got out of the lightweight class, myself. I was tired of being beat up."

A little way down the slope Lieutenant Angsberg kicked at the loose snow at the side of the road while he looked anxiously at Jeremiah Potts. Angsberg was a couple of years past twenty and this was his first fight. He'd joined the regiment at Couteaux as a replacement for Lieutenant Pat Zambriski, who'd been killed on the Roer. The platoon didn't know much about Wilmer Angsberg; they looked at him a little askance and Wilmer felt their reserve and it worried him. He worried about things, anyway.

"I'm pretty new at this, I guess," he said to Potts, peering through his steel-rimmed spectacles. "Oh, I know about tanks and all that, I suppose. But I've

never been in a real fight before, Captain. I
wouldn't want to make a mistake."

Jerry Potts chewed on a fir twig, his round, good-
natured face placid. He was ten years older than
Wilmer. In civil life he'd been a professional ar-
ranger of conventions. He considered that he'd already seen practically every type of behavior genus
Homo was capable of producing and nothing surprised him any more.

"I wouldn't worry about it," he said. "Once
you've been in a fight five minutes you'll think
you've been there all your life. At least I did."

Wilmer looked more worried. "Sir, can I ask you
a question?" He blurted the words, his face red-
dening.

"Sure. Ask away."

"Were you scared before your first fight?"

Jerry Potts looked at Angsberg with mild astonishment showing in his chubby face. "Chum," he
said, "I've been scared before all of my fights. I've
been scared during them and I've been scared after
them. That's the way you keep alive in war."

Angsberg looked a little relieved. "Thanks, sir,"
he said. "I thought it was just me."

The radio squawked in the scout car and the
operator answered — then handed the mike to Potts.
"It's the Old Man, Captain," he said. "He wants to
talk to you."

Potts spat out the fir twig and said, "Potts, sir,"
into the mike. "Over."

"Where are you?" Boone's voice asked.

Potts gave him the map coordinates in code; he

added that they had a pretty good position and were remaining in observation. They could see about a mile east along the Maastricht road. So far, the column they had spotted earlier hadn't showed up.

"I was out ahead of the tanks with the scout car, sir," Potts said. "I don't think the Germans saw me and I hauled foot back here pretty fast."

"Good," Boone said. "I'm on my way up there. Stick where you are until I arrive. Out."

Jeremiah Potts passed the handset back to the operator in the scout car and looked at his watch. It was five minutes before seven in the morning — rainy and cold. Sergeant Butch Marcus was gesturing to him from the V in the ridge. The day's chores were about to begin, Potts was thinking without any particular emotion as he turned towards the ridge, Angsberg beside him.

Task Force Prebble was forming up the road, tank drivers red-eyed and tired and full of bad humor after last night's march. At the head of the column Miles Boone spoke with Lieutenant Colonel Bill Prebble. The latter was a slender, profane man who moved with a quick and nervous energy. Like Boone he had been a cavalryman before the war and the two had known each other casually.

Boone passed on the information Potts had given him. "Get your outfit up there as soon as you can, Bill," Miles said. "I'm going on ahead. I'll meet you there."

"That's the trouble with this war," Prebble

fumed. "It keeps the hours of an idiot owl! Half of my men haven't even been fed yet. Okay, sir, we'll whip our nags along."

Boone nodded and was turning away towards where Lute and Corporal Millikin waited in the jeep when he saw McCrumm coming at a trot through the rain. He waited until the infantryman reached him. The latter didn't bother with formalities.

"Rafferty's getting hit hard," McCrumm said. "Armor and infantry. So far he's holding but the tanks could cause him trouble. If you could spare some tank destroyers we could use them."

"I'm releasing a platoon of tank destroyers to you," Boone said. "Tell Nash those are my orders. I'll be back here as soon as I find out what is developing on the Maastricht road."

"Right," McCrumm said.

"Any word yet from your first and third battalions?"

McCrumm shook his head. "Not yet. I've got people out looking for them. If they got overrun, stragglers ought to be drifting back in here by now."

Boone nodded and slid into the jeep beside Lute. Behind him drivers were gunning the tank engines of Task Force Prebble. The warming effects of the coffee Lute had found for him were dying out now and fatigue wrapped him like a sodden overcoat. He fought it away as he grunted at Lute.

"Let's go."

This wasn't the way to do it, he knew, as the

vehicle's tires skidded in the slushy snow, then caught with a jerk that flung him back against the seat. He was dissipating Combat Command B piecemeal; he was nibbling it away, a bit here and a bit there. If you went by the books it was all wrong. And yet what else could he do? It looked as if Rigny would shortly be under attack from three sides and he had to build his hasty dams the best way he could. Later he'd try to pull in the pieces.

And the worst of it was that he had no reliable information as yet. He was like a blindfolded man striking in all directions against a swarm of hornets he couldn't see.

Beside him, Lute Heard was mumbling savagely as he hunched over the jeep's wheel, holding the swaying vehicle to the road. The mumblings increased Boone's irritation. Confound it all, he had enough on his mind without Lute Heard acting like a fool prima donna, he decided crossly.

"Either say it out loud or shut up!" he snapped.

Lute glanced at him briefly out of the corners of his eyes, his unshaven cheeks further reddened by the rush of the cold wind. Somewhere in Rigny, Lute had found a dirty purple scarf and had tied it around his neck so that the ends flapped loosely.

"All right, I'll say it!" Lute growled. "When are you goin' to learn to stay put like a general is supposed to do and stop scally-hootin' all over the country like this?"

"When I can find some way to get the job done better," Miles said through his teeth. "Do you know one?"

"I could name a dozen," Lute snarled. "What are you looking for — glory? Or just tryin' to get us both killed?"

"If you don't like it you can go back to Fort Knox," Miles said roughly. "I told you that once before."

Lute's voice suddenly became more pacific. "Aw, nuts," he said. "You know what I mean, Miles. Old Blocker's already chewed you out for running off doing a captain's job. Why not stay back in Rigny while you send Prebble up here?"

"Because I've got to find out what's going on," Miles said, his own voice losing its edge as it lapsed back into tiredness. "And the best way to do it is to go where it's happening. Maybe it's not according to the book but I've got a feeling that all of the books in the world aren't going to be of very much use to us for the next few days."

"All right," Lute said soberly. "I got my answer — I'll keep my mouth shut from now on."

In the back of the jeep, Corporal Millikin clung to the rail and looked at the backs of the two in front of him with shocked eyes. Corporal Millikin had never heard a sergeant talk to a general like that before. It was turning colder. Little runnels of rain froze on the stock of Lute's M-1 in its scabbard lashed to the windshield post. The jeep was fleeing down a long slope which climbed to a low ridge beyond when the *spang* of a tank gun put its flat crack into the morning air.

Jerry Potts, crouched behind brush at one side of

the ridge's V, watched through field glasses as a German armored car cautiously poked its nose out of the trees on the white skyline a mile away. It stayed there a moment, its turret swinging from side to side as an animal sniffs the wind. Then it moved boldly out into the road, followed at intervals by two more.

"Company," Potts said, chewing on a new fir twig. "Want a look, Loot?"

Angsberg, crouched beside him, took the glasses. They were not quite steady as he held them to his eyes and Potts noted the fact with mild amusement. Heavier stuff was showing through the trees there now and he took the binoculars out of the lieutenant's hands again.

"What are those big ones?" Angsberg asked.

"Tigers. Mean babies. Real mean."

"Should I . . . shouldn't I start firing on them?" Wilmer asked, trying to make his voice sound casual but not quite succeeding. "I mean they ought to be in range."

"Don't be so bloodthirsty," Potts said. "Wait until they get sort of spraddled out across that bridge. The ground's too soft for them to get off the road — we ought to be able to sting them a little there."

"Sting them?"

"A Sherman's gun don't worry the frontal armor of a Tiger much," Potts said drily. "Catch them on the bridge, though, and there'll be a lot of milling around and you can get in a shot at a track or ammo rack. Leave it to Marcus — he knows the trick."

"Oh," Wilmer said vaguely. "I see. Suppose that

general doesn't come with help like he said he would. What do we do then?"

"Run like crooks," Potts said cheerfully. "Come on, let's get back to the tanks. The curtain's about to go up."

Butch Marcus still stood in the hatch of his tank, disdaining to button it up. Across the way, Second Lieutenant Wilmer Angsberg also stood, not quite certain just what he was supposed to do. The three German armored cars already had crossed the bridge and were moving toward the V. A. Tiger tank edged onto the bridge with another following. Wilmer looked at Butch who made an O with his thumb and forefinger.

"Fire!" Wilmer said, his voice too high.

Steve Reilly's gun was the first to let go. It belched fire, the racket clapping Butch's ears. The shell exploded against the front armor of the leading Tiger, wrapping the turret briefly in flame. Confusion took hold of the column there as the leading tanks began to back and turn.

"Maybe you didn't hurt him but I'll bet that you scared him into the green fantods," Marcus yelled down to Reilly. "Try for his ammo rack now that he's turning!"

"So now you're trying to teach me my business," Reilly yelled back. He added, speaking to his loader, "Give me high explosive this time, Yacob."

The other tanks were firing now and the explosion of Reilly's gun was lost in the ragged crashes. A pinpoint of light glowed behind the turret of the turning Tiger; then the whole vehicle was wrapped in flame as ammunition went up with a great swoosh. As the smoke cleared Butch saw that it was burning furiously.

"Nice shooting," he said, his voice sober now.

"Heil Hitler!" Reilly answered through his teeth.

The armored cars were beating a hasty retreat towards the bridge. A shell from a Sherman caught one of them squarely, slicing through the thin armor to explode within. The armored car veered crazily across the road and tipped down into the ditch and started to burn. A single dark figure scrambled free of the wrecked machine and started to run heavily across the snow. Butch Marcus' machine gun cut him down as he ran.

Most of the German column was pulling back now to the screen of the trees on the far skyline but four Tigers had maneuvered into position on ground that was solid and were returning the fire of the platoon in the V. The shells were high at first as the partial defilade of the low crest protected the Shermans. Butch was beckoning frantically to Angsberg to get down in the hatch and button up. He was too late.

A high velocity shell landed squarely in front of the turret of Angsberg's tank and red-hot metal scythed across the hatch where Angsberg had been standing. He fell forward, his body almost cut in half, as a second shell landed. The Sherman became a blazing funeral pyre. Second Lieutenant Wilmer Angsberg had not had a chance to know long how it felt to be in battle.

A fragment of the exploding shell had gouged

Butch Marcus across the cheek and he was swearing fretfully as he ducked under cover and pulled the hatch doors shut. At his feet Reilly and Yacob loaded and fired with a stolid deliberation. Across the way another of the Tigers slued drunkenly as an exploding shell broke its right-hand track. The remaining three began to retreat along the road, firing as they went. Presently their firing ceased.

"Let 'em go," Butch said. "We got no ammo to waste. The lootenant just bought it, Steve. No. 1 tank went up like a big Roman candle."

Reilly's face was grimed with powder smoke. "This platoon's hard on lieutenants," he said, but there was no levity in his voice as he sagged loosely on his steel seat.

Butch Marcus opened the hatch again and climbed slowly out. He did not look at No. 1 tank, which was still burning, as he dropped down into the snow. He was the senior tank commander left and he had command of the platoon now, he guessed; he wished that he didn't. A jeep had stopped by the scout car behind the crest and General Boone was talking with Captain Potts. Butch went towards them, his steps lagging.

Miles Boone had his plan ready when Task Force Prebble arrived at the ridge twenty minutes later. The road ahead of the V was empty except for the knocked-out vehicles by the bridge, but long-range fire was coming from the trees on the far skyline. As yet it had done little damage.

The remaining four Shermans had pulled farther back behind their own crest and the flat trajectories of the high-velocity German tank guns sent the shells over to burst harmlessly in the empty fields beyond. That wouldn't last long, Miles knew. The German commander would be hurrying self-propelled artillery up to place plunging fire on the notch.

He'd hold here along the ridge for the time being, Boone had decided. His own 105-mm howitzers could reach the far skyline and keep the German column disorganized. If the German heavy tanks tried the road again, the 90-mm guns of his tank destroyers would be able to take care of them; the ground beyond the road was not yet frozen hard enough to allow German armor to maneuver off the highway. The company of armored infantry, dug in along the ridge, could prevent German infantry from infiltrating forward.

He issued his orders to Prebble in terse sentences as the two of them stood in the rain. A high-explosive shell burst in a clump of woods to the left of them and twigs and fir needles showered down to make a green carpet on the snow. The 105-mm howitzer battery had already gone into position and, as Boone spoke, its first salvo half drowned his words. The armored infantry company was moving past them towards the ridge.

"Is everything clear, Prebble?"

"What about the tanks?" Prebble asked.

"Keep them out of it," Boone said, "unless the Germans try an all-out push down the road. I don't think they will — not until they've felt you out and softened you up a bit with artillery. That won't be until afternoon, anyway."

Prebble jerked his head in his swift, nervous gesture. "I got it. How long do we stay here?"

Fatigue lent sharpness to Boone's voice. "Until I tell you to get out," he snapped. Then his tone eased as he put a hand on Prebble's arm. "I'm going back to organize some sort of a defense of Rigny, Bill. You've got to buy me time up here to do it in. That answer your question?"

Prebble grinned wryly and wiped the rain off his face with his sleeve. "Yes, sir," he said. "I guess that that's all the answer there can be."

"It is — Get going and good luck."

Captain Potts was coming up from the scout car as Prebble left. The usual benign expression of the S-2's face was a little worried as he stopped beside Boone. The latter regarded his staff officer abstractedly, his mind still on the thousand-and-one things that had to be done if Rigny was to be held.

"Well?" he asked.

There was a faint apology in Potts' voice. "I was just talking to Leroy Jefferson on the radio, sir," he said. "He told me that another German armored column has been reported moving towards Rigny from the south along the Eifel road. Leroy said that Colonel Nash requests orders."

It's like a runaway forest fire, Boone thought without any particular emotion. You stamp it out in one place and it flares up in a new spot miles away.

To Potts he said, "Message to Nash. He is to move south at once, pick out a blocking position and hold off the German advance until further orders. Get that to him, Potts. Then follow me. We're going back to Rigny."

No rifle fire had crackled yet from the ridge but the 105 howitzer battery was firing slowly and deliberately as the jeep pulled out, followed by the scout car. The crash of the cannon seemed to tear the gray morning apart; it echoed from the hills like the beat of great gongs. The pattern that he must follow was taking shape, Boone was thinking as he rode beside Lute Heard, only dimly aware of the acute discomfort of his sodden clothes. One thing was certain. He couldn't hold Rigny against converging German columns all spraddled out the way he was.

He'd have to organize a defense of the town itself, using what was left of McCrumm's regiment as it filtered in, using the stragglers he'd turned back last night, using Combat Command B as he was able to pull it back from its blocking positions. It would take time. He could only hope that the two task forces he had sent out could buy him that time before they were too badly mauled to be battle-worthy....

His head was nodding as the jeep bounced over the slick road. He shook his drowsiness angrily away but it came back, pressing down on him like a heavy hand. Lute Heard's voice lifted sharply but the words were blurred and far away and they made no impression on Boone's drugged mind.

"Hang onto him so he don't fall out," Lute snapped to Corporal Millikin. "An' let him sleep. He's got it coming to him, the poor buzzard."

Snatches of dreams made crazy patterns. They began in the middle and ended in the middle as dreams do. There was the boxing room back at West Point with the afternoon sun coming through the windows to make bright patches on the floor.

A voice was saying, "Why don't you give it up, mister? You know you can't lick me . . ."

"I'll keep coming at you," another voice said.

That dream went away and he was back in the kitchen of the big farmhouse outside Couteaux. Firelight made a little flicker of dancing shadow on the walls. There was a blanket-covered table with a poker hand on it, face up. Aces and eights. The dead man's hand.

Then Janet de Ceilly's soft voice came to him clearly from beyond the shadows. "It's been such a short time, hasn't it, Miles? So terribly short."

There was something that he must ask her — something very important. It kept eluding him and he was angry that he couldn't remember what it was. Another voice, growing clearer, broke into his consciousness. Lute's voice.

"I hate to do this to you, Miles," it said. "Wake up. We're back at Rigny again."

A half hour later Miles Boone walked into the

schoolhouse where McCrumm still had his command post. Steaming coffee and a K-ration heated in its can had put new life into Boone. That hour of uneasy sleep, caught in the wet seat of a jeep bouncing over a chuck-holed road, had worked wonders. If he'd just had time for a shave, he was thinking as he went up the schoolhouse steps, he'd feel right on top of the world.

McCrumm, his own face stubbled and his uncombed hair standing on end, was sitting at a table littered with maps and papers as Boone came in. McCrumm started to get to his feet but Boone waved him back and came to sit on a corner of the table. McCrumm looked up at him with wry eyes.

"You look like the cat that just ate the cream, General," he said. "Maybe you've got some good news that I haven't heard yet. Most of what I've had has been bad."

Miles grinned tightly. "I just got an hour's sleep in a jeep, drank about a gallon of coffee, and downed a can of what the quartermaster blithely calls a meat-and-egg product. Even *that* tasted good. You ought to try it sometime, Colonel. It's surprising how tasty hunger can make it."

McCrumm ran a hand through his hair and there was a faint surprise in his eyes. This was a side of Boone that he hadn't seen before, he was thinking. Maybe this hard-rock, driving general was human beneath his hard shell after all. McCrumm would like to think so. He respected and admired Boone;

up to now the idea had not occurred to him that he might like him, too.

"Maybe I will, sir," McCrumm said. "Nash got your orders — he moved south toward Eifel three-quarters of an hour ago. No word from him yet. Is the situation up where you were turning out okay?"

Miles nodded. "For now, at least. What about Rafferty?"

"Still hanging on. They've been catching it rough but they're still there. A captain named Ziegler brought what is left of the first battalion in about an hour ago. They were overrun yesterday — battalion commander killed, executive missing, about the strength of two companies left. I've got Ziegler reorganizing it back in town. Filling it up with stragglers."

"Good," Boone said, his light mood dissipating as he put on the mantle of responsibility again. "What about your third battalion? Anything?"

"Not much. A few stragglers have been coming in from the south. Maybe a hundred of them all told. The third was overrun, too. All the men I've talked to are pretty vague about it — nobody is sure just what happened. Ziegler's using them also to help fill up the first battalion."

Boone said, "Good," again and there was high approbation in his voice now. He'd not been mistaken in McCrumm, he was thinking; he had a good man here. A man who did things without being told. "All right — here's the plan."

He outlined briefly the things that he had decided

on up at the notch. A defense of Rigny that began at the outskirts of the town and took advantage of the soft ground that would channel the German armor into the restricted approaches of the roads; a defense that would use the houses of Rigny as cover for McCrumm's riflemen and its streets as avenues of counterattack for the tanks of Combat Command B.

It was a little before noon now. By dark they should have their hasty defenses pretty well set up. After dark the three covering forces would fall back to the town. Given any luck at all, they should be in pretty good shape by tomorrow morning.

Some of the tiredness seemed to go out of McCrumm. "I never thought this place could be held," he said. "Maybe I'm crazy but I'm beginning to believe now that it can."

Boone looked down at him with no expression on his dirty, finely drawn face. "It's going to be held, McCrumm," he said. "One way or another, it's going to be held."

"Yes, sir." McCrumm got to his feet and reached for his helmet. "I'll give Ziegler the dope — get him started to picking out positions for strong points . . ." he began.

"Not yet," Boone said crisply. "You're going to get some coffee first. And some food. After that, sack out for an hour. Go over to my command post. Lute Heard will take care of you. That's an order, Colonel."

"Nuts, General, I'm not . . ."

"I'll take over while you're gone. Beat it."

McCrumm went, weaving a little from fatigue. Doggone if he didn't almost like this general, he was thinking, the temporary release from responsibility acting on him like a tonic. He did like this general, he decided.

It was early afternoon when Miles Boone, Lute Heard with him, completed his reconnaissance of the town. It was better adapted for defense than he had hoped. There was one flaw in his plan, he knew. If the ground should freeze hard tonight — or tomorrow night or the night after that — the German tanks would no longer be restricted to movement on the roads. They could come at the town from across the fields, and that would be a horse of another color. Well, he'd worry about that when he had to, Miles decided.

The jeep came into Rigny's main square. Men milled about here as they had yesterday but now there was some sort of order to their movements. That captain — what was his name, Ziegler? — must be reorganizing McCrumm's first battalion somewhere hereabouts, Boone decided. He'd have a look at the man.

At Boone's word, Lute stopped the jeep. A building across the square, a shop of some kind from its windows, seemed to be the center of activity. Miles told Heard to wait and started for the building. He passed a sign, crudely lettered, which had an arrow reading: C.P. — 1ST BATTALION.

Boone climbed to the low stoop and was about

to enter the door when he was shoved aside by a
muddy, unshaven man who seemed to be going
somewhere in a great hurry. A drawling voice,
whose Southern accent carried a deadly note, followed from inside.

"An' the next time, Sahgint," it was saying, "don't
you take up my time with no fool excuses."

Miles went in. It was a square room with a
serving counter and shelves that had been cleared
of bottles; tables and chairs were stacked untidily
against a far wall. One table still stood in the
room's center and a man sat there, his head bent as
he scrawled on a piece of dirty paper with a stub
of pencil. He didn't look up as Miles moved toward
him.

"What you want now?" he asked in the drawl
Miles had heard. "Whateveh it is, you can't have it.
Confound it, cain't you learn you got to hustle for
yourself in this wah?"

"I'm General Boone," Miles said.

The man looked up. He was about twenty-five,
Boone guessed, and he had blue eyes deep-set in
a mournful face beneath a shock of fiery red hair.
For a moment he regarded Miles with a mild interest; then he leisurely unfolded his long, lank
frame from the chair and stood up. He wore torn
G.I. trousers and a German officer's leather coat on
which a captain's bars had been pinned. A faint
pleasure showed in his face now.

"The heck you say," he said, coming around the
table to thrust out a bony hand. "Ah'm Bud
Ziegler frum Texas, seh. Ah reckon I'm right glad

to meet you. Never expected to see no generals up heah, I got to say."

There was something very likable about this slow-moving Texan, Boone decided, as he felt the other's hard handshake. He remembered the muddy sergeant who had passed him at the door and thought that he understood now how Captain Bud Ziegler had been able to bring in what was left of the first battalion.

He mentioned that briefly and saw the pleasure in the other's face again. "Doggone Germans kind of ruckused us yesterday, General," he said a little apologetically. "When it come dark, we was two miles from where we was supposed to be an' all sprawled out like a stepped-on aig. We had Germans all around us so I figured I better bring the boys here an' find out what it was all aboot. So I brung 'em and here we are, seh."

Boone looked at the leather overcoat. "You had to fight your way back?" he asked.

"Yep," Ziegler said placidly. "It was a kind of a to-do. If youah wonderin' about the coat, General, I borrowed it from a German. He didn't have no use for it no more."

Boone smiled tightly. "I don't imagine he did," he agreed. His tones turned clipped again. "How are you coming along with reorganizing the first battalion?"

"Right sma't, seh. Cou'se I got me a slew of rear area replacements — ordnances an' quartermasters an' medics an' like that. They wasn't too happy 'bout being made into doughboys but I sort of

convinced 'em. Wouldn't be surprised if they didn't
do right fair. We stickin' heah in Rigny, seh?"

"We're sticking," Boone said. "I'm going to need
your first battalion, Captain. Have it ready." ·

"It'll be a pleasure, General," Ziegler said. "The
boys are real upsot about gettin' kicked around up
nawth the way they did. We got a lot of fight left in
us yet."

"Good," Boone said. "I'll see you."

Major Summer, Potts and Jefferson with him, was
in the room which had been turned into an operations office when Miles got back to his command
post. The major, who had sweated off some of his
fat in the last three days, was staring at a slip of
paper in his hand, a worried look on his red face.
He turned, his eyes showing relief, as Boone came
through the doorway.

"I was just about to send Potts to look for you,
sir," he said. "A message from division has just
come in."

Boone took the slip of paper — stepped to a window where the gray light of the afternoon came in.
The message was short and to the point. The rest
of the Hammerhead Division had been diverted to
the south of Brey to stop a German penetration
there. Combat Command B would hold Rigny at
all costs. That last was repeated. *At all costs.* The
message was signed "Blocker."

Boone stood for a moment, looking out into the
fading daylight. Clouds, heavy and dark and ominous, seemed almost to touch the tops of the firs

on the low ridge he could see from the window. He hoped that there would be more snow tonight; if it snowed there would be less chance of a freeze. He was conscious that the three in the room were looking at him questioningly as he turned back to them.

"This seems to be clear enough," he said, showing a poker face as he handed the message back. "Gentlemen, we stay here. Has there been any word from Colonel Nash?"

The message center chief answered the question as he came hastily into the room. "One just come in, sir. Colonel Nash says they're gettin' hit by an all-out attack. He don't think that he can hang on much longer, sir!"

"Tell him I'm on my way," Boone said. "Lute . . ."

Sergeant Heard came, the dirty purple scarf still wound around his neck, and he and Boone went out together. Boone paused for a moment on the porch, sniffing the air. The wind was from the north and he thought that the day was growing colder. Lute shivered, his face looking more pinched than ever.

"If I ever get back to Kentucky, I hope I got sense enough to stay there," he grumbled. "This climate is for the birds! Well, where we goin' now?"

"To Nash's outfit. He's in trouble."

"It figures. Tell me when he wasn't!"

Six

TASK FORCE NASH had set up its blocking position
in a little hamlet, not shown on the map, through
which the road from Eifel ran northward. As Miles
Boone and Lute Heard rode into the place, German
artillery was methodically knocking the half dozen
houses into rubble. The tiny village lay at the bot-
tom of a shallow bowl under direct observation
from the low ridges to the south. Why Nash had
picked the place, Boone didn't know. They'd passed
at least two better positions on the way here.

The road was cratered with shell holes and Lute
gingerly steered the jeep around them, swearing
under his breath as he did so. At the aid station, a
hundred yards to the rear in a small woods, an
overworked medic had said that the command post
was up front in one of the houses, he thought.

"I wish . . ." Lute began.

The sentence was never finished as he jammed
on the brake and dove out of the jeep in a long
fall, Corporal Millikin close on his heels. Boone
went out of the vehicle's other side. A high screech,
like the whistle of an onrushing express train, grew
to a shrieking crescendo in the dying afternoon.

The shell exploded in the road ahead of the jeep, a great belch of black smoke laced with red. Lethal fragments buzzed like angry hornets as Miles Boone felt something like a fist slug the calf of his right leg.

The echoes retreated and Miles could hear Lute Heard complaining in an ill-tempered monotone on the far side of the jeep. He sat up, dizzy with the concussion of the bursting shell as he shook his head to rid himself of the ringing in his ears. The stink of burned powder was acrid in his nostrils and little tendrils of smoke still curled up from the hole which had been blown in the pavement. He was lucky to be alive, he knew.

He remembered the fist that had slammed against his calf and looked down at his right leg. One of the high-buckled leather boots, which dated back to his cavalry days, had been cut across as cleanly as if it had been slashed by a razor. He leaned forward and pulled the three-inch slit open with his fingers; his underwear was cut but only a fine thread of blood showed against the skin of his leg. The shell fragment had barely scratched him.

He called, "Lute, are you all right?"

Heard's voice, frustrated and shaky with pent-up fury, came back from the jeep's far side. "I'm all right. Millikin ain't. Blast those buzzards!"

Boone hauled himself up and moved across the road, limping a little as his bruised leg pained him. Heard was hunkered down beside Corporal Millikin, a hand inside the other's field jacket. A glance at the corporal's face — at the dark stain which was spreading along the left side of the field jacket — told Miles that it was no use. He was sorry. He had grown to like the curly-headed radio operator with the serious face and the solemn eyes. He reached a hand down to Lute.

"Come on, Lute," he said. "You can't help him now. We've still got work to do."

The jeep's engine was still running and Heard parked it behind one of the houses where a half dozen stiff figures lay, blankets pulled up over their faces. Boone made his way down the road, keeping close to the buildings. He passed a Sherman, burned out but still smoking. Two armored infantrymen, manning a machine gun that poked out from a second-story window of one of the houses, looked down curiously as he went beneath.

A telephone line, snaked along the ground, led him to the last house and he paused there, sitting on his heels, while he looked at the snowy fields beyond. The road ran straight to disappear in the dark trees on the crest of a low ridge beyond. Dark patches dotted the snow like piles of old clothes carelessly thrown away. Two tanks and a scout car were in the ditch on either side of the road, their guns tilted at useless angles.

Nash had been fighting here.

Nevertheless, there was little sign of the "all-out" attack that Nash had reported over the radio — of German pressure so great that Task Force Nash was unable to hang on where it was at least until dark. Certainly at the moment things were quiet enough except for German shellfire coming from beyond the ridge. Boone's lips flattened out thinly and his face looked darker and more saturnine as he stepped into the building.

Rubble covered the floor; furniture and clothes were carelessly scattered. He made his way to the rear where a yellow light shone from stairs leading to a cellar. He went down the steps, wondering if Nash had failed again; unhappy with himself because he hadn't followed his first hunch and relieved Nash from command back at Couteaux.

An oil lamp, resting on a shelf, threw smoky yellow light across two officers bent over a table where a field telephone stood. One was a lieutenant colonel whose name Boone didn't remember but who, he knew, was the executive of the armored regiment. The other was a captain also unknown to him. Both of them straightened to a wary attention as Boone came towards them.

"Where's Colonel Nash?" he asked sharply.

"He's not here, sir," the lieutenant colonel said inanely. Miles had his name now — it was Robertson. "He's with the armored battalion. That is, he accompanied it."

"And where's the armored battalion?"

The wariness deepened in Robertson's face. "Would the general look at the map, sir? I could explain it better. Colonel Nash's plan, I mean."

"All right. Show me."

Robertson's words were hurried, stumbling on

each other, as he traced a line on the map with his finger and tried to explain. Colonel Nash was convinced that the Germans were massing for an all-out attack, he said. Earlier, Nash had noticed this farm road on the map which led through the woods to high ground overlooking the Eifel road beyond that crest to the front. Captain Aulbe, here, had reconnoitered the secondary road and found it firm enough to take the weight of the medium tanks.

"How far did you reconnoiter it?" Miles interrupted savagely. "Until you got to the high ground?"

A sense of impending disaster had suddenly added a new weight to his shoulders. The sound of fresh firing reached the cellar. The increased tempo and the sharper crashes could mean tank guns going into action, Boone thought. The idea didn't make him any happier. Captain Aulbe looked scared.

"No, sir," Aulbe said. "There wasn't time to go all the way because Colonel Nash thought that the German attack might come any minute and he had to have the information fast."

"How far *did* you go?" Miles asked through his teeth.

"About a quarter of a mile, sir."

"How about the ground on either side of this secondary road? Was it hard enough to take the weight of tanks?"

"Tanks couldn't get off the road there, sir. The trees are too thick and . . ."

Boone shut the captain up as though a hand had been slapped across his mouth. When he spoke again, his voice was furious.

"Captain," he said, controlling his anger with an effort, "I just pray that you and Colonel Nash haven't cost us one battalion of tanks. Of all the . . ."

He stopped, his habitual poker expression coming back into his dark face. The harm was already done and he'd have to hope for the best; it wouldn't help any to take out his anger on these two over Nash's foolhardy rashness. What had possessed the man, he wondered. To put a column of tanks on a narrow road where it couldn't maneuver — couldn't even turn — was the height of folly. Only an empty-headed glory hunter would take such an insane risk in the face of an enemy like the Germans.

The man thinks he must live up to the Nash name and be a hero, Miles raged inwardly. He's got to lead a charge at Gettysburg or gallop up San Juan Hill like the other Nashes have done! And he costs me a tank battalion I can't afford to lose!

None of his thoughts showed in his face, though, as he turned abruptly on his heel and headed for the stairs. Lute was waiting for him just inside the doorway of the house. Boone told him curtly what had happened. They would have to get the battalion back here if they could.

"A glory boy," Lute said softly. "I thought I seen it in him the first time I laid eyes on the guy. I told you a long time ago to tie a can to him, Miles."

Boone scowled. "Never mind the I-told-you-so bit," he said sharply. "Where's the jeep?"

Lute shrugged and led the way out into the rubble-littered street. Despite the increased firing from beyond the ridge, no shells from tank guns were landing in the village, Miles noted, and that increased his uneasiness. It must mean that German armor was engaging his lost tank battalion.

Lute had lifted Corporal Millikin's body and placed it beside the others in the blanket-covered row behind the wall. Neither man spoke of it as they climbed into the jeep, freshly scarred by shell fragments. Lute started the engine and wheeled back into the road. The afternoon was far along and it was starting to snow again, Miles noted with a faint relief.

At least that was a break. There would be no hard freeze tonight to make solid ground out of the fields and permit German armor to move where it pleased.

Some three miles up the secondary road Colonel Nelson Nash was having second thoughts about the plan that had seemed so dashing, so in keeping with the cavalry tradition back there in the village. Nash rode in a jeep at the head of the tank column and right now he was becoming unhappier with each passing moment. The conviction was growing in him that he might have put his head into a noose by coming up this road.

For the past half hour the track had led through

fir woods which became thicker and thicker. The trees, snow-hooded, stood so close together on either side of the road that no tank could butt its way through; it was doubtful, Nash realized with growing concern, that the big machines even had room to turn around should he decide to reverse the column. A somber twilight, into which snow was again beginning to fall, hung here in these woods and increased the gloominess of his thoughts.

Unpleasant thoughts, each an accusation. No room to maneuver or deploy. If this road should suddenly debouch in sight of the Germans, the battalion would be a sitting duck with no more fire power to it than that possessed by its lead tank. Something close to panic gripped Nash as the lead weight in the pit of his stomach became heavier and more icy cold.

He'd had nothing but bad breaks!

A little self-pity was beginning to erode his thoughts. That knuckle-headed operator who had garbled his radio message to Rigny, for example, had reported erroneously that the Germans were attacking heavily and that Task Force Nash might be forced to withdraw. The message that Nash had meant him to send was to the effect that heavy German attack was imminent, probably in such strength that it couldn't be held.

"The blasted fool!" Nash said involuntarily now.

The jeep driver looked at him out of the corner of his eye as the vehicle crawled along the snowy and rutted track beneath the gloomy firs. "Sir?" the driver asked.

"Nothing," Nash snapped impatiently. "Pay attention to your driving, Sergeant!"

Of course, he'd sent out a corrected message as soon as he had learned of the mistake. But it had been too late. Boone had already left, they had said. That had been another bad break because he'd had no illusions about what *that* hard-rock general would do when he arrived at the blocking position and found out what the true situation was.

It was then that the idea of this flanking operation had occurred to Nash. He'd already noted on the map the secondary road leading to the ridge and he'd had no doubt that the German armor *was* massing behind the ridge for an all-out attack along the Eifel highway. If he could hit them in the flank with his own tanks before their attack got started he would hurt them badly, perhaps cripple them to the point where they were no longer a threat to Rigny — at least for today.

On impulse he had ordered the tank battalion to march, himself at its head. It was the sort of thing his father would have done, he had told himself. Now he wasn't so sure.

The rutted road swung more toward the south and wasn't so steep now. Nash shook himself out of his lethargy and looked back. The big Shermans, snuffling and growling, were coming on through the trees, tank commanders standing in the turrets, drivers guiding the heavy machines skillfully along the narrow way. A thrill of pride lightened Nash's thoughts for a moment.

The jeep driver expelled his breath in a half sigh. "I think we're comin' out on the ridge, Colonel," he said.

Nash turned back to the front, the tension suddenly easing in him. The woods were thinning out and there was high ground visible on either side now. Maybe this was going to pay off after all, he thought as excitement ran through him.

He signaled back for the lead tank to halt and to pass the signal on. "Hold it up," he said to his driver. Over his shoulder he told the radio operator to get word to Lieutenant Colonel Bradbury, the battalion commander, to come up.

Nash was standing in the snow, his carbine slung, when Bradbury arrived. The latter was a short, chunky man with sardonic eyes. He didn't bother to salute.

"Trouble?" he asked shortly.

"The top of the ridge is just ahead," Nash said, not bothering to keep the exultation out of his voice. Bradbury earlier had voiced a sharp disapproval of this plan. "Come along, we're going up on foot to have a look."

Bradbury spat. "Okay," he said. "I hope to John it's more open there than it is here. These trees are beginning to give me claustrophobia, I don't mind saying, Colonel."

They moved on for a hundred yards as the ground gradually flattened and the woods became less dense. Another fifty yards brought them to the spine of the ridge where another shallow valley fell away in front of them. Nash's hand suddenly tightened on Bradbury's arm as both dropped to the snow.

"Look!" Nash said.

He unconsciously lowered his voice to a whisper. His guess had been right. To the south the ridge fell away into a little saddle and, on its far side, half a mile away, German tanks made squat, dark shapes against the snow. They were tightly grouped and not buttoned up, their crews wandering about or squatting beside their vehicles while they smoked and talked.

Bradbury grunted deep in his throat. "Sitting ducks," he said. "What we can do to 'em! I never had much faith in this scheme, Colonel. I guess I was wrong."

Nash felt his excitement mount. "Bring up the first two companies, Bradbury," he said, fighting to keep his voice steady. "Deploy them just out of sight behind the ridge. Make it as quiet as you can. The wind is blowing away from them and toward us but we'll take no chances."

"We'll come like little mice," Bradbury said.

"Odd-numbered tanks will fire armor-piercing shell," Nash went on, his voice confident and sure now. "Even numbers, high explosive. The crews are on the ground and that should keep them from manning their tanks."

"Right. Anything else?"

"Nothing. When you're in position I'll give the signal for the advance. Make it fast."

"Right!" Bradbury said again and went back down the road at a loping run.

The next fifteen minutes seemed like centuries to Nash as he crouched in the snow, watching the German armor assembled across the way. At any second he expected to see the crewmen running for their tanks, either because they'd gotten some warning of the threat to their rear or because they'd been ordered to the attack along the Eifel road. Behind him the racket of his own tanks coming up seemed a thunderous clatter which the Germans surely must hear. The cold wind was blowing hard but in spite of it he wiped sweat away from his face. Repeatedly he looked impatiently back to see if Bradbury was in position.

Finally the stubby man waved both arms over his head to signal that all was ready. Nash let his breath go out explosively as he stood up and swung his own arm forward. Tank engines thundered into full life and clattering tracks tore at the snowy ground as the Shermans surged forward the last few yards to the ridge.

"Fire!" Nash was yelling.

Tank guns flamed. It wasn't war. It was execution. High explosive shells, bursting among the massed vehicles eight hundred yards away, scythed unprotected men down like the blades of a reaper. Armor-piercing shells penetrated the thinly protected rear of tanks, setting gasoline afire

and exploding their ammunition. Minutes after the
first Sherman fired, the far slope of the saddle was a
blazing inferno out of which a few men ran crazily
— but only a few. Columns of black smoke, laced
with flame, erupted violently as more tanks exploded. It was soon over.

Nash found that he was running along the line
of his own tanks yelling, "Cease firing! Cease
firing!" in a voice that couldn't be heard. The
firing stopped because there was nothing left to
shoot at. Bradbury came to stand beside Nash,
sweat beading his face.

In an awed voice he said prayerfully, "What a
mess! What a mess!"

Nash understood what he meant. He, too, was a
little shaken by the work of his guns. It took him
several seconds to think what he should do next.
Then he remembered that gloomy road guarded
by the scowling firs.

"Get the column on the road again," he said
to Bradbury in a normal voice. "We're going back."

The tanks were moving again, their metallic
clanking filling the semi-twilight, when Nash saw
the jeep. It was coming toward him, dodging in
and out among the forming vehicles. Lute Heard
was at the wheel; Miles Boone sat beside him. Nash
squared his shoulders and waited for them.

He'd be casual about this, he decided. He'd give
Boone every chance to let himself down easily.
After all, he could afford to be generous now.

The jeep stopped a dozen feet away and Boone

stepped down, speaking a curt word to Heard who stayed behind the wheel. He came on toward Nash, his gait neither hurried nor slow, and his face showing nothing. As he reached Nash he halted and his hard glance took in the destruction across the way. Still he did not speak and the silence now began to ride Nash.

"Nice shooting, don't you think?" he asked finally.

"Nice shooting," Boone said, his voice flat and impersonal. "I imagine you knocked out about the equivalent of a battalion over there. Would you say that?"

"I estimate it that way, sir."

Boone turned away from the scene so that he was facing Nash squarely now, the last of the daylight outlining the angles of his thin face. "And how many battalions of armor would you estimate the Germans have converging on Rigny, Colonel?" he asked, still in that impersonal tone. "Twenty? Fifty?"

Nash looked startled. "I don't know, General," he said, a faint irritation beginning to run in him at this line of questioning. "I never gave it much thought."

"I didn't think that you had," Boone said, an edge coming into his voice now. "If you had maybe you would have remembered that we have only *two* and you wouldn't have risked one of them on a hundred-to-one shot that fortunately was lucky enough to come off!"

A slow red was beginning to creep into Nash's face. This wasn't fair! He'd pulled off a smart tactical move; he'd taken a calculated risk and he'd won! If you won, that was all that mattered, wasn't it? He started to say that.

Boone cut him off. "I know all about that hooey that anything in war can be forgiven if it is successful," he snapped. "In my book it doesn't apply. You deliberately jeopardized one of our two tank battalions by taking it into a defile where it could neither maneuver nor deploy. Under certain circumstances a calculated risk is all right. Under these circumstances it was not. It was about as wrong as anything can be!"

"But . . . ."

Again Boone cut him off. "There's a story that goes way back, Nash. Maybe you will remember it. It's about a gunner on a ship who, through his negligence, allowed a gun to break loose in a storm. It charged along the deck endangering the whole ship until this same gunner, at the risk of his life, managed to get it under control again. Do you remember the end of the story, Nash?"

"I remember it," Nash said sullenly. "The captain of the ship decorated him. Then ordered him shot."

"Do you see any parallel between that story and what has happened here this afternoon, Nash?"

"I do not," Nash said, anger making his voice hoarse. "You've ridden me ever since you came to Combat Command B, General. I'm tired of it! I formally request that you relieve me of command and prefer charges against me. I think that a court-martial will take a fairer view of this than you have!"

For a moment Boone didn't answer as he stood studying the man before him in the fading light. The tank column was starting to move back down the secondary road now, the sound of the tank engines muffled by the trees.

"I meant to relieve you when I started up here, Nash," Boone said finally. "I have changed my mind. You're a West Pointer. You've been a professional soldier for twenty years. Your country and the Army has a right to expect a return in the investment made in you. You are going to continue to command this regiment . . . and from now on you will do it right."

Night had fallen and it was snowing more heavily when Miles Boone got back to Rigny. McCrumm was waiting for him and together they toured the defenses that had been hastily thrown up around the town. They weren't perfect but they'd do, Boone decided. There was never a time in war when you had all that you wanted.

"Tell Rafferty to disengage and start moving back at 2200," he said to McCrumm. "I'll pull my two task forces back at the same time."

"Joe's dead," McCrumm said tonelessly. "He got it about an hour ago—shell fragment through the chest. Oliver will bring the battalion out. He's a good man."

Boone put a hand out and touched the other's shoulder. "I'm sorry," he said gently. "He was your friend?"

"We grew up together," McCrumm said gruffly as though he feared to trust his voice. "It's going to be hard on his wife. She's a good kid."

"I'm sorry," Miles said again.

He moved away through the snowy darkness. It's often the good ones who go, he was thinking. It's hard but that's the way it will always be, for it is the good ones who offer themselves at the point where the danger is greatest. All at once he felt very lonely as the snow brushed against his face.

He wondered what Janet was doing now. He hoped that she wasn't worrying but he knew that she was. Would the Germans get as far west as Couteaux? He didn't know; he didn't suppose that anyone knew for sure. Well, it was the war. . . .

The command post seemed warm and cheerful after the cold and wet outside. Boone dictated orders to Summer for the withdrawal of his two task forces; waited in the operations room until the message center chief returned to say that they had been dispatched and acknowledged. Lute Heard came in.

"How about some chow?" Lute asked gruffly. "You look like you could use it."

Miles nodded and got up. What he'd really like to do, he was thinking, was sack out and sleep for twenty-four hours. His mind dwelt fondly on the idea as he followed Lute back to the kitchen of the house. It was the most attractive idea that he had ever had, he decided. Things were quiet now. Maybe he could grab a couple of hours.

It seemed to Miles that his head had just touched the blanket when someone was shaking him awake. In the light that came through an open doorway he saw that an orderly was bending over him. It wasn't Lute Heard this time.

"General," the man was saying, "Task Force Nash is starting to come in. You said to wake you up . . ."

"Okay, son," Miles said thickly. With an effort he sat up and swung his feet to the floor. "I'm awake. Put on a light and then see if you can find me some hot water, will you?"

The orderly lighted a kerosene lamp and went back through the door as Miles ran a hand through his close-cropped hair. *What was that crack I made to Lute back at Couteaux?* He grinned wryly as he answered his own question. *It's a young man's war. Well, you're learning that for yourself, Boone.* He grunted at the stiffness in his joints as he began to pull on his boots.

The orderly — just a kid — came back with a wash basin and a steaming pitcher of water as Miles was fastening the last of the boot buckles. In the yellow light of the lamp the shell slash across the leather of the right boot gaped widely and the soldier stared at it with round eyes.

"Gosh, General, you get hit?" he asked.

"Nope," Miles said, suddenly cheerful despite the sleepiness that was still in him. "That one passed me by."

"I'm sure glad," the orderly said.

For some obscure reason the remark pleased Miles more than he had been pleased in a long time. "Thanks, son," he said. "I'll remember that. You can go now."

He shaved, reveling in the luxury of hot water and a face that was free of mud and grime for the first time in two days. It was ten minutes later when he donned his helmet and went to the operations room. Jeremiah Potts had the watch. He got to his feet, his round face placid, as Boone came in.

"Everything quiet?" Miles asked.

"All okay, sir," Potts said. "We had a message from Colonel McCrumm a little while ago that his second battalion had disengaged successfully and is on the way back. Task Force Nash is starting to come in. Colonel Prebble's outfit should begin to arrive in another half hour."

"Good!" Miles said. "I'm going to the Eifel road to meet Nash. Can you dig me up a driver for my jeep? I'll let Heard sleep for awhile. He's not as young as he used to be."

"I heard that," Lute Heard's voice said sourly from the kitchen door. He stalked across the room with disdain, yanked open the outer door, said, "Horse feathers!" vindictively over his shoulder, and slammed the door behind him.

"Well, I asked for that," Boone said ruefully.

Jeremiah Potts grinned. "Sergeant Heard is a pretty salty character, sir," he said. "From what I've seen, we could use a lot more like him."

"He's a good man to have around," Miles agreed soberly. "Send for me if there's anything new, Captain."

He followed Lute out into the night and stood on the stoop for a moment, his eyes accustoming themselves to the darkness as he tried to read the weather. It had stopped snowing but the sky was still heavily overcast so that no starlight came through. He thought that it was colder, but the overcast was a good sign. Clear skies would bring the freezing weather that he didn't want yet.

Lute, still cranky and uncommunicative, stopped the jeep off the Eifel road near the edge of town. A little knot of men stood in the shadows and Miles went towards them. Nash was there and, at Boone's word, joined him as the two stood apart from the rest and talked in low voices. A stream of vehicles went by them, entering Rigny.

"Have any trouble?" Miles asked.

"None, sir." Nash's voice was distant and formal. "We disengaged without incident."

"How about casualties?"

Nash enumerated them, men and vehicles, in that same flat tone. His voice was sure and he had no need to consult a slip of paper this time, Boone noted with satisfaction. "We brought our dead back with us," Nash concluded shortly.

"Good," Miles said in a toneless voice.

He issued orders as to how Task Force Nash would dispose itself in its new position. Its mission was to defend the southern sector of Rigny where the Eifel road came in. One of its tank companies would report to Lieutenant Colonel Ike Garton, commanding the reserve. It would tie in on its left with McCrumm's second infantry battalion which would defend the eastern approaches to the town. Were there any questions?

"No, sir," Nash said stiffly. He stepped back, saluted and started to turn away.

Boone's voice halted him. "You've done a good job in getting back here tonight, Nash," he said.

The other's voice was icy. "Yes, sir," it said.

It was midmorning, a cold wind blowing, when the first German attack came. It hit down the Maastricht road—not directly from the east as Boone had expected. He headed for the northeast sector, Lute driving and a new radio operator riding in the back of the jeep. Boone's mind checked over the town's defenses for a final time as he rode.

He'd inspected the semiperimeter at first light this morning. Men, working all night, had dug in the tanks and the tank destroyers at places where they had the best fields of fire possible; the supporting field-artillery batteries were sited behind the town where they would have a certain amount of defilade and the houses would not mask the fire of the howitzers. Machine guns had been emplaced and bazooka men stationed where they could do the most good. Prebble commanded the northeast sector; McCrumm, reinforced by a company of tanks from Prebble's battalion, had the center; Nash commanded the south of the town.

Ike Garton held the Combat Command reserve near the center of Rigny. He had his own armored infantry battalion, less the two companies detached to the task forces, a company of tanks, Bud Ziegler's makeshift infantry battalion, and some other odds and ends. Not the best set-up in the world, Boone was thinking, but the best that he could devise under the circumstances.

He had violated all doctrine as to how tanks should be used, he knew. Tanks should be kept mobile for use as a striking force; they shouldn't be dug in to serve as gun and machine gun emplacements. Every book said that. But the book didn't fit here at Rigny. Here only one thing was certain — Rigny must be held. He'd have to improvise as best he could to do it.

Prebble's command post was in a house near the northeast edge of town and Boone followed the lieutenant colonel up the stairs to where a sandbagged window gave a view of the rolling terrain in front of them. Last night's snow lay white and clean on fields dotted with clumps of firs. The road, running straight as a string here, dipped out of sight behind a fold in the ground a mile away; it reappeared again to be swallowed by a wooded skyline two miles farther on. Tanks and trucked infantry, looking like black bugs against the snow, crawled along the distant section of the road at widely separated intervals.

"Those birds are well within artillery range, sir," Prebble said hopefully. "Stan Kowansky has been worrying at me for the last half hour for a target."

Boone shook his head. "Not yet," he said. "Wait until they show their noses over that last ridge. Then have Kowansky put a concentration down on the road behind."

A section of the division trains had accompanied Combat Command B on its march south from Couteaux, carrying ammunition, gasoline and rations, but there was no telling how long it would be before any resupply could be made, Boone knew. He couldn't afford to waste precious ammunition sniping at individual tanks with his field guns. He'd wait until his target was sure.

It was 1010 when the first Tiger tank nosed over the ridge ahead. It was followed by four more, men riding on their hulls behind the turrets. A moment later another group of tanks, Panthers, not as heavy as the Tigers, appeared on the high ground to the left of the road. Infantry moved with them as they advanced cautiously down the slope. Still another group, tanks and infantry, showed on the road's right.

Prebble looked questioningly at Boone. "Your baby, Colonel," the latter said and Prebble left for the stairs at a run. An instant later the first American tank gun fired. Miles saw the shell explode harmlessly against the heavy frontal armor of the leading Tiger lumbering down the road.

They're gambling that the ground is hard enough to hold their Panthers, Miles was thinking. If it is, we're dead ducks. If it isn't, we've got a chance—until the first freeze.

The Tigers were firing now — 88-mm shells which tore into the town. One of the Panthers was hit. It slued around on the slope, its spinning tracks unable to get traction on the soft ground. It was hit again and began to burn, a dark pall of smoke climbing into the sullen December sky. Infantry spilled away from the flaming tank and machine-gun fire from the town went out to meet it with the vindictiveness of mad hornets.

Beyond the ridge other columns of smoke were rising as Combat Command B's 105 howitzers began to lay down their concentrations. Miles watched. There was nothing else he could do now, he knew. Prebble was doing all that could be done. Lute Heard's face appeared at the head of the stairway.

"McCrumm says half of the German army is comin' at him along the east-west road," Lute grunted. "He thinks maybe you'd ought to get over there."

Butch Marcus, disdaining his periscope and standing in the hatch of his dug-in tank, shouted directions to Reilly. The Sherman was well to the

left of where the Maastricht road entered Rigny so
that it could deliver a degree of flanking fire. The
leading Tiger was within four hundred yards of
the first houses.

"Now!" Butch said.

The Sherman's 75-mm gun spoke. Almost simul-
taneously the shell exploded with an orange flash
against the partially exposed track of the German
tank. It wheeled sharply to its left as its driver
tried to control it. It nosed down into the ditch, its
gun pointing at a useless angle. Men spilled from
behind its turret and deployed across the snow.

"Them babies ain't runnin' — they mean business," Butch said to no one in particular. "I guess
you better get with it."

He yanked at the handle of the machine gun. It
began to jump beneath his hands as his steel-jack-
eted slugs searched the snow, the tracers winking
yellowly. Reilly fired at the second Tiger and
missed.

"I taught you better than that," Butch yelled
down to him. "You're makin' me look bad, pal."

"He ducked," Reilly said and fired again.

Orange flame flared just behind the turret of the
second Tiger. The orange was swallowed by a bigger, brighter flash as the ammunition exploded in
the rack. The tank slued around, partially blocking
the road, while smoke seeped from its ports. A
moment later it was wrapped in flames as its gasoline caught fire. The other tanks came on.

"They must be stupid," Butch grumbled. "Don't they know by now we don't like 'em?"

It was the last thing Butch ever said. Up the white slope the long snout of an 88, ugly with its bulbous muzzle brake, swung deliberately as its gunner trained it on the dug-in Sherman that he had just spotted. He pressed the firing lever. The high velocity shell smashed through the turret armor of the *Fayetteville Floozy* as a sharp knife cuts through cheese. A great light filled the whole of Butch Marcus' world. That was the last thing he saw.

Battle flamed all along the eastern edge of the town. Woods approached more closely here and the rolling ground gave the attackers better protection. Two companies of *Volksgrenadiers* gained lodgement in the houses to the left of the east-west road a little before noon. Captain Bud Ziegler, leading his ragtag battalion, routed them out again but not without cost.

Boone met Ziegler as the latter was on his way back to the reserve position. One sleeve of the expensive leather coat, which had once belonged to a German officer, had been slashed to the shoulder so that it flapped loosely. Blood from a deep cut smeared Bud's face along with powder smoke, but the captain's eyes were as imperturbable as ever.

"Howdy, General," he said.

"How'd it go?"

Ziegler gave Miles a mournful regard. "Real ole

tom-cat of a scrap, seh. We whup 'em, though. Them are right good boys that I got, General."

"Yes," Boone said. "They're good boys. Rest them all you can, Ziegler. I'm afraid they are going to be pretty busy from now on. Pretty busy."

"Shouldn't wondeh," Ziegler said laconically, waving his hand in a vague salute. "See you around, seh."

Firing suddenly broke out at the southern edge of the town. Task Force Nash was engaged, Boone knew as he turned in that direction. Rigny was under assault from three sides now. Rough. He climbed into the jeep and Lute Heard let out the clutch. They rolled through streets beginning to fill with rubble from the shelling, and went toward the Eifel road. It was early afternoon.

The viciousness of the German assault waned as the short twilight died and darkness came down. Rigny still held. Twice more during the afternoon the reserve had been called on to counterattack against local penetrations. Sporadic tank attacks still came in but the pressure was eased a little. Except for the shelling. That grew steadily heavier as the Germans, angered by their delay in taking this town which lay astride their main roads of advance, brought up heavier stuff to hammer home a steady harassing fire. It inflicted mounting casualties. Worse, Miles Boone thought, it kept the handful of defenders from getting any rest.

He had moved the location of his command post

nearer the center of town to be closer to his reserve. A shell had exploded in the street just outside, leaving a gaping crater and loosely flung cob-
blestones. He skirted the hole and went into the
house whose lower windows had been shattered
by the blast. Captain Jefferson was speaking on
the field telephone. He finished and put the handset down and stood up. A scrap of paper was in
his hands.

"Message from General Blocker, sir," he said.

For a moment Boone's heart leaped. That could
mean that the rest of the Hammerhead Division
had been released from its former assignment and
was on its way to Rigny now. Then a glance at
Jefferson's face told Miles that he was just kidding
himself — that the news was not good. A glance
at the message confirmed that and he felt the fatigue grow in him.

FROM BLOCKER TO BOONE. IMPERATIVE YOU HOLD
RIGNY UNTIL DARK TWENTIETH TO PREVENT EN-
CIRCLEMENT OF BULK OF TROOPS STILL EAST OF
VAAR. DIVISION IS HOLDING BRIDGEHEAD AT BREY.
RETIRE ON BREY UNDER COVER DARKNESS TWEN-
TIETH. CAN SEND NO HELP.

Boone put the slip of paper down on the table.
"Captain," he said to Leroy, "what day is today?"

Jefferson looked worried. "The seventeenth, sir."

"I was afraid of that," Miles said. "You don't happen to have any weather prophets in your family, do you?"

The worry increased in Leroy Jefferson's long, lantern-jawed face as he moved his big hands nervously. "My granddaddy used to know when it was going to rain, sir, by the way his corns hurt," he said in an embarrassed voice.

"Too bad he isn't here," Miles said, forcing a faint grin. "Maybe he could tell us whether or not it's going to freeze. It would be a help to know."

Seven

AFTERWARD Miles Boone could never clearly remember all the details of the three days that followed. Neither could the other defenders of Rigny — those who lived through it. Those days and nights were a monstrous illusion in which men moved automatically as though they were in the grip of a nightmare. A nightmare made up of furious attacks of German armor and infantry against the perimeter, of the crazy laughter of machine guns, of the crump of mortars and of shells that fell ceaselessly like an iron rain. A nightmare of aid stations filled to overflowing and of burial parties that worked in the night.

And still the German attacks came in. They hammered out of the mists of the mornings; they were gray wraiths that came out of the snow which intermittently fell. The defenders of Rigny went to meet them, stubbled, hollow-cheeked men who fought with the ferocity of wildcats. And still it didn't freeze and still Rigny held, but by paper-thin margins.

A dozen times a day the dwindling reserve, like an overworked fire brigade, dashed to threatened points to plug the gaps. Ike Garton, commanding the armored infantry battalion, died of wounds on the evening of the second day. Boone promoted Bud Ziegler to major on the spot and gave him the command. He could depend on the lanky Texan, he had found.

McCrumm's second battalion, reinforced by stragglers, still held on the east-west road but it was eroding away. Both Task Force Nash and Task Force Prebble were down to two-thirds of their original strength but they fought on. Bill Prebble was out of the fight, badly wounded, and Monk King commanded the Maastricht sector but the task force still wore Prebble's name.

An exploding 150-mm shell blew the jeep out from under Miles Boone just after daybreak on the morning of the third day. For a moment he lay against the wall of the house where he had been flung, the taste of blood in his mouth and his head swimming from the concussion. Lute Heard lay in the snow a dozen yards away. As Boone's vision began to clear he saw Lute sit up.

The expression on the sergeant's red, hatchet-sharp face was one of disgusted disbelief as he carefully felt each leg — then each arm. Finally he stood up and gingerly patted his belly as he came toward Miles. The latter was on his feet now, leaning against the wall as his head cleared. There was blood on his face where a shell fragment had slashed his cheek.

"You all right?" he asked Lute.

Heard spat disgustedly. "I get blowed halfway to Jerusalem an' back and I don't even get a Purple Heart out of it," he said. "I never seen such a fouled-up war. You look like something the cat drug in — we better hunt up an aid man."

The morning, which had been fairly quiet up to now, suddenly came alive with the racket of gunfire to the south. They were hitting Nash again, Boone thought. Another day's chores had begun. The blood from the slash in his face was dripping off his chin and making a mess of the front of his field jacket.

"Find us another jeep," he told Lute. "I'll get this cut patched up and meet you on the Eifel road."

Lute looked mournfully at where the jeep made a heap of scrap in the street. "I was gettin' fond of that bucket," he said. "It'll be like breakin' in a new horse."

He clumped off through the snow, Boone watching him go for a moment. It had been close, he thought; Lute had just about used up his store of luck. Maybe he should make him stay at the command post. He smiled a little grimly as he started down the street to where Ziegler's reserve was. Lute stay away from a fight? That would be the day, he decided. It never occurred to him to think that maybe his own luck was running out.

Bud Ziegler squatted on his heels beside Boone in the front room of a house ventilated by shells as an aid man cleaned the wound in Boone's cheek and taped it up. Tawny stubble covered Ziegler's dirty cheeks and a bandage around his left forearm showed through the torn sleeve of his leather coat. Weariness showed in the sag of his shoulders but his eyes were still bright and curious and his drawling voice serene.

"Yes, seh," he was saying, "I figure we got it made, General. Jest a few moah hours to hang on — then we skeddadle foah Brey an' the Germans can have this town. Me, I wouldn't take it as a gift if you was to throw the rest of Belgium in."

The aid man said, "That ought to hold it, General. It ain't a first-class job but I'm about out of stuff to work with. Business has been kind of rushing."

Boone looked at the row of wounded lying in the hall and at buckets overflowing with the grim, stained refuse of the aid man's trade. Then he looked back at the aid man himself, really seeing him for the first time. Deep fatigue lay in the other's gray face and dark splotches dyed his clothes.

"It's fine," Boone said. "You've been doing a good job here, son. I won't forget it after we get out."

"General, you think we're going to get out?" the aid man asked, his eyes brightening a little.

"Of course we're going to get out," Miles said sharply, getting to his feet. "And we're taking our wounded with us. You can pass that word along."

The aid man's eyes were still brighter. "Now I think those guys'll be right glad to hear that," he said. "Yes, sir, General, I'll pass the word along."

It was still quiet at the northeast corner of the town as the day began to grow. Out in front the snowy fields were empty except for the heaps, partially snow covered, where vehicles that had been wrecked in the three days' fighting lay. Sergeant Shultz crouched in the shelter of No. 3 tank while he spooned cold K-ration out of a can and argued with Corporal Tinker, his driver. The argument was about religion this time.

"Every man's got some sort of a religion," Tinker was saying, his long face earnest. "It stands to reason that he has. Everybody's got to believe in something, Sergeant. He'd be no better than an animal, if he didn't."

Shultz chewed without pleasure on his mouthful of meat-and-egg mixture. Behind the two, shells crumped down into Rigny. Fifty yards away lay the ruins of Butch Marcus' burned-out tank. Butch had been a friend of Shultz's.

"You think Butch had a religion?" he asked through his mouthful. "He ever say he had?"

"He never said it to me," Tinker said stoutly. "Just the same, I'll bet he did."

"You think he's some place up in the sky right now, setting on a cloud an' picking a harp?"

"I do."

Sergeant Shultz spooned the last of the K-ration into his mouth, looked distastefully at the empty can and tossed it away. It made a tinny sound as it struck the dug-in tank and rolled away in the snow. Shultz swallowed the mouthful with an effort and searched for a cigarette. He took the last one out of a crumpled package and regarded it stolidly. From now on he wouldn't be smoking, he knew.

"Maybe you could be right, Tink," he said. "I'd kind of like to think it, anyway. Butch was a pretty good guy."

"I liked him," Tinker said.

Both men fell silent for a moment as they listened to the crash of shells behind them in town. Out in front the white fields looked peaceful beneath the lowering sky except for the wrecked vehicles and the black scars on the snow left by exploding shells. Sergeant Shultz dragged the smoke of his cigarette deep into his lungs and shifted his position as he looked at Tinker out of the corners of his eyes.

"Maybe it wouldn't do no harm, Tink," he said, his voice a little too offhand, "if you was to read a couple of passages out of the Book. It'd sort of be nice to hear."

Tinker nodded, a glow of satisfaction on his thin face. He took the Testament from an inner pocket and carefully undid its oilskin wrapping. He held the small volume in his hand and allowed it to fall open where it would. Ellsworth, the cannoneer, and Feeley, the bow gunner, came up silently to crouch down behind Shultz and Tinker.

"The eighth chapter of Romans, the eighteenth verse," Tinker said solemnly and read:

For I reckon that the sufferings of this present time are not worthy to be compared with the glory which shall be revealed in us.

Tinker read on, his voice slow and solemn as it had been when he had read before the congregation in the church back home in South Carolina. Two or three men from the armored infantry company drifted by and stood listening, mixed expressions on their faces. Tinker finished and began to rewrap the Testament in its oilskin.

"Amen. Much obliged, Tink," Sergeant Shultz said, his voice gruffer than usual. Across the way, a German tank poked its heavy snout above the ridge line. The day's work was about to begin. "Looks like we got business, boys."

In the early afternoon the fury of battle died down a little and Miles Boone assembled his commanders at the command post in the center of Rigny to issue orders for the withdrawal that night. Nash came last. There was little about him that resembled the smartly dressed officer of a few days before. Whiskers covered his cheeks and his helmet was dented and his trousers torn and caked with mud. A dirty strip of tape crisscrossed his face. A few minutes earlier he had personally led a counterattack and destroyed two tanks that had gained lodgement in the town.

He closed the door behind him and walked a few paces forward to halt and salute stiffly. "Colonel

Nash reporting, sir," he said, his eyes bleak on Boone's face.

"Fall out," Boone said tiredly. "Find yourself a place to sit down, Colonel."

"I prefer to stand, sir," Nash said in a cold voice.

He hates my guts, Boone thought. I don't suppose I can blame him. Just the same, he's a lot more of an officer now than he has ever been before.

"Suit yourself," he said in a voice just as cold.

His eyes swept the faces of the others in the room: the infantryman, McCrumm, with his left arm in a sling; the commanders of the field artillery battalions who had been suffering counterbattery fire for the last three days; Bud Ziegler, the reserve commander, who leaned against the wall.

"The order to withdraw after dark tonight still stands," Boone said. "We move southwest toward Brey. Major Summer has a schedule showing the times that each of you will disengage and indicating your position in the march column. The reserve, Major Ziegler commanding, will cover your withdrawal and form the rear guard. I will be with the reserve. Any questions?"

There were few. These men were too tired, too spent to have any deep thoughts or to quibble over details. It was enough for them that they were leaving this evil place tonight. They had fought a good fight and they knew it. They need feel no shame at abandoning it under orders.

"Very well, that is all, gentlemen," he said after

a minute. "Colonel Nash, will you remain a moment?"

They filed out and Miles waited until the door had closed behind the last of them. Nash was still standing at a strict attention in the center of the room when Boone finally turned to him; the colonel's face was bleak and his eyes stony.

"Nash," Miles said, "at Couteaux I told you that I thought you had let your family name down — worse, you had let Combat Command B down. I make no apology for those words. I want you to know now, however, that I consider your conduct of the past three days in defense of Rigny soldierly in every way."

"Thank you," Nash said stiffly.

"Would you care to shake hands, Nash?"

"I would not," Nash said.

He saluted, his face looking as though it had been cut from stone. Then he faced about and marched with a deliberate step towards the door. It closed behind him.

Boone's expression was dark and musing as he went to the window and looked out. The gray day was lighter than it had been, he noted absently; that could mean that the weather was clearing and that it would freeze tonight. He was sorry that Nash had refused his overture but he had no intention of worrying about the matter. Lute Heard came in, his grin sardonic.

"I was listenin' at the door," he said blandly.

"Got your hand spit in, didn't you? Maybe some day you'll learn."

"One of these days that curiosity of yours will get you an ear pulled through a keyhole," Miles said without rancor. "I'm moving with the reserve tonight. You'll take Summer and Potts with you in the jeep and march with Nash's column."

"Like heck I will," Lute said crossly. "Me and the jeep will be right along with you. I've brung you this far — I don't aim to lose you now, by grab!"

By a little after 2100 all three task forces had stealthily withdrawn from their positions at the edge of town and were beginning to move on the road toward Brey. As they had drawn back, units from the reserve had taken their places to form a thin shell about Rigny. Mission: prevent any German probing attack from discovering that the town was being evacuated. The artillery remained in position, firing until the last moment.

The next two or three hours would be the critical ones, Miles knew as he stopped at the schoolhouse that Bud Ziegler had taken over as his command post on the east-west road. Combat Command B, and the orphans it had picked up, needed that much time to get free of the town and well on the road. If its departure were not discovered — pursuit started before midnight — the chances were that it could reach Brey and the bridge across the Vaar unmolested. That was his reason for staying here.

He heard desultory firing to the northeast as he

stepped through the blanketed door and went down the hall to the room on the right. Ziegler was talking on the field telephone.

"Now, you ain't goin' to let a couple of little ole tanks skeer you, aire you?" he was saying as Boone entered. "You go right out there, Joe, an' chase 'em away."

He put down the handset and looked at Miles with a mild pleasure. "Howdy, General," he said. "Place seems kind of lonesome, don't it, with all the boys gone this-away."

Miles slouched in a chair, putting his helmet on the table beside the field phone while he scowled at the helmet's single star. Tension had been building up in him during the past hour; something that hadn't happened before during the four days he had spent here at Rigny. Even when the German attacks had been at their worst he had never had any doubt that Combat Command B would hold. Now, however, it was different.

A vague foreboding troubled him, a feeling that something disastrous was going to happen. He tried to shake the feeling away. Across the table Bud Ziegler was regarding him with melancholy eyes.

"Trouble?" Boone asked, jerking his head at the phone.

"Naw," Bud said in an unbothered voice. "That was jest Joe Metzger. He seen a couple of Tiger tanks comin' down the road an' they spooked him. Joe spooks easy."

"How about the other outposts?"

"All quiet, General, seh. One thing you can say about the Germans — they're real methodical guys. When the quittin' whistle blows, they knock off for the night."

"I hope so," Boone murmured.

The field telephone burred again and Ziegler scooped the handset to his ear. "Yeah?" he said. He listened to squawking noises that came from the other end for a moment. Then he said, 'I'll be there," in a voice quite different from his usual lazy drawl and put the handset down again.

"Maybe I talked too soon," he said to Miles. "That was Johansen out in front of here. He says German searchlights are lightin' up his position like it was Broadway and he can hear a slew of tanks. I reckon I better get up where I can see what's goin' on, General."

"We'll both go," Miles said.

Ziegler looked vaguely disturbed. "Why don't you jest set here by the phone, General," he said. "I'll give you the word as soon as I get it. Knockin' off tanks ain't a general's job."

Boone reached for his helmet. "Let's go," he said.

Ziegler stood up, his face more melancholy than ever. "I git a general shot an' I'll never live it down," he said. Then he called in a louder voice, "Willie, you come guard this heah phone. Me an' the general is goin' up front."

Miles Boone looked at his watch as he and Lute Heard and Ziegler crouched behind the hasty barricade that had been thrown across Rigny's main street. Behind them lay a little square where the street divided into the roads running west to Vaaracre and southwest to Brey. The last two and a half hours had been filled with vicious fighting. Step by step the reserve had been forced back through the town, pressed hard by the Germans who sensed that they were about to crack this stubborn nut at last.

German infantry had infiltrated the narrow streets; German tanks, their machine guns yammering, prowled like big cats through the night seeking their kill. There was nothing but dog-tired, hurting infantry left to Ziegler's reserve now. All of the tank company's Shermans had been knocked out. One tank destroyer remained but it had no ammunition for its big 90-mm gun and so fired its last machine gun from the shelter of the barricade.

The Germans had set fire to the houses in the eastern part of the town and now the night, turned clear and cold, held a ruddy glow which was reflected on the faces of the square's defenders. They'd shot their bolt, Boone knew. To stay here longer would be suicide for those who were left.

"Time to go," he said to Ziegler.

"I was hopin' you'd say that," Bud grunted. "Me, I got my bellyful of fightin' for one day. I'll go pass the word to the boys, what ones is left."

He was starting to get to his feet when a man,

his helmet gone and a dirty, bloodstained bandage wrapped around his head, came out of the shadows and crossed the square at a shambling run. The eerie half-light from the fires washed his face briefly as he dropped down beside Ziegler.

"Major," he said, panting from his run, "they've got two tanks in back of us. They're workin' their way up that street by the church . . ."

Ziegler said to Lute, "Sergint, you had a bazooka in yoah jeep a little bit ago. Git it!"

"Never mind!" Boone said sharply. "Get your men together and start them moving back on the Brey road. Tell them to scatter and go cross-country if German armor pursues them. The ground's still not frozen enough for it to get off the road."

"But, General, them tanks . . ."

"Heard and I'll take care of them. Come on, Lute. Let's go." They got the bazooka from the jeep. Boone tucked its tube beneath his arm as Heard picked up the three rockets that were left. Boone grunted, "Not many. We'll make them do."

They kept to the shadows as they carefully worked their way toward the church. This wasn't in the books, either, Boone guessed; a general hunting tanks with a bazooka. Still, it was better than sitting around doing nothing, he supposed.

Lute said sourly at his shoulder, "They should have kept you locked up in the Pentagon! I used to think that only some generals was crazy. Now I know they all are!"

"Scared, Lute?"

"You just bet I'm scared!" Lute snorted. "I got good sense, ain't I? Well, here's your fool street!"

Miles stepped into it — jumped back as machine-gun fire swept it, the bullets screeching off the cobbles. He waited until the firing stopped; then poked his head cautiously out again. A little thread of elation was beginning to run through him like a tonic. He was starting to enjoy this war for the first time, he decided; instead of having to send someone else out to fight, he was doing a little fighting on his own now.

The street was narrow — barely wide enough to admit the two Panther tanks that were crawling toward him a hundred yards away. In the red glow Miles could see them as they came, the second following the first at about twenty-five feet. They were squat and wicked-looking, with the big noses of their cannon poking ahead. His puny rockets wouldn't even dent their frontal armor, Boone knew; he had to get a shot at a track or ammo rack.

"There's an alley up a little ways," he said to Lute. "We'll ambush them from it."

He sprinted around the corner, the bazooka tube banging clumsily against his leg. Machine-gun bullets chased him. Then he was into the shadows again, Lute beside him mumbling under his breath. The growl of diesel engines and the clank of steel treads were coming closer as Miles balanced the bazooka on his shoulder and squinted along the barrel.

"Been quite awhile since I shot one of these," he said to Lute in a conversational voice. "Be fast with those rockets — we've got to be sure of stopping the first one. That'll block the street to the second."

"You just pull the trigger — I'll tend to the loading," Lute said without enthusiasm. "And you better remember to duck if that big baby turns its cannon in here."

He slid a finned rocket into the breech of the bazooka, latched the breech and tapped Miles on the shoulder. The muzzle-braked snout of the lead Panther's cannon showed in the mouth of the alley. Then the tank's side was there. Miles sighted on the tracks and pressed the firing device and it seemed to him that the world went up in flames as the blast of the exploding rocket hit him from fifty feet away.

He staggered back, bracing himself against the wall as he saw the Panther stop and its long turret gun start to turn. Lute was tapping his shoulder again.

"Clear!" he was yelling.

Miles was aiming behind the turret at the ammunition rack now. He fired just as the turret gun flamed — knew that he had missed as the explosion of the cannon shell in the narrow space flung him backward, nearly tearing him apart. The bazooka was lying a dozen feet away and he crawled towards it, stopping to get the last rocket from Heard who was face down on the cobbles. It seemed to Boone that it took forever to get the bazooka loaded again but the job was done at last.

He got shakily to one knee, aiming a long time as he tried to hold the sight steady on the tank's hull where the ammunition rack was. Once more he crooked his finger. There was a brief *whoosh;* then the world went up in fire. Concussion belted Boone like a giant sledge as consciousness left him.

Awareness seeped slowly back into Boone. He opened his eyes and the glaring light intensified the pain which was tearing his head apart. He lay on the floor of a room where two men were talking in guttural voices. He listened, thankful now for the German he knew. He was a prisoner, and the thought made his head hurt worse.

Obersturmbannführer Holtz would be here soon, one was saying. No doubt he would be greatly pleased that they had captured an American general. An American general could be very useful — and think of what propaganda it would make!

Miles fought down the nausea which suddenly threatened to engulf him. *Obersturmbannführer* meant an SS lieutenant colonel, he knew; a dedicated Nazi who respected no rules except his own and Hitler's. Things could be bad when he arrived. Well, to heck with it! He didn't intend to play dead, Boone decided stubbornly.

He pulled himself up, propping his back against the wall. Lute Heard lay beside him, his eyes closed and his breathing heavy. As his vision cleared he saw two German soldiers looking at him curiously in the light of a gasoline lantern which stood on a table in the center of the room. They didn't speak.

Footsteps sounded outside and the door was flung violently back as a slender officer of about his own height and build entered the room. SS Lieutenant Colonel Holtz, Boone guessed by the other's insigne. The officer snapped a curt command to the two soldiers and they went out, closing the door behind them as Holtz crossed the room. He stood above Miles, feet spread apart and hands on his hips, as he spoke excellent English.

"So, you are the American swine who has held us up at Rigny for four days," he said harshly. "You are going to regret that before we have finished with you, I think."

The line of the Nazi's mouth and the harsh arrogance of his voice convinced Boone that he wasn't listening to an overstatement. He wished that the pain in his head would let up so that he could think better as he stared back, his own eyes hard. His tone matched that of Holtz when he answered.

"I'll tell you my name, rank and serial number, you Nazi dog," he said in a brittle voice. "Nothing more."

Holtz's voice was mocking. "We already know your name, rank and serial number, Brigadier General Miles Boone. We also know you commanded Combat Command B of the Hammerhead

Armored Division. You may be interested to hear
that a German officer, resembling you and dressed
in an American uniform with your stars and
identification, will be parachuted into Brey before
daylight. When he has finished certain tasks there,
your name is going to be quite famous, I think,
General Boone."

Again nausea surged over Miles Boone as the
full implication of this thing hit him. A counterfeit
American general, issuing false orders, could ac-
complish more harm than could a panzer division
in the confusion which must exist back on the Vaar.

"You can't get away with this!" he said hoarsely.

"I fancy we can," Holtz said, his voice still mocking. "Meanwhile, you will answer certain questions, General."

"I'll answer nothing!"

"In that case we will take this swine out and
shoot him," Holtz retorted harshly, jabbing the toe
of a polished boot — not gently — into the ribs
of Lute Heard. "We will also shoot you but not
until . . ."

He didn't finish because Lute suddenly uncoiled
like a spring as he sat up, his hands going out to
grab Holtz's leg while he sank his teeth in just
above the knee. Holtz swore viciously and bent
to get his hands in Lute's hair. It was all the op-
portunity that Miles needed. He struck twice with
the edge of his hand, *karate* chops that found their
target, and Holtz dropped like a poleaxed steer.
Strength was coming swiftly back into Boone as

he jerked the German's pistol from its scabbard.

"Thanks, Lute," Miles said briefly as he got to his feet. "I owe you one for that."

"I don't like a boot in the ribs," Lute said sourly, spitting and rubbing his side.

Miles bent and felt for Holtz's pulse. There was none. He had not expected that there would be. He reached down to Lute and helped the other man to his feet. "He's said his last Heil Hitler, Lute."

"Okay. What do we do now?"

Miles gestured him into silence as a voice called in German outside the door. Miles answered sharply, imitating Holtz's arrogant tones with a fair degree of success. The voice outside answered respectfully and feet scraped as the questioner went away. The conversation had given Boone an idea as he laid the pistol on the table and began to unbuckle the dead Holtz's belt.

"I never knew you could talk German," Lute said without enthusiasm. "What the devil you doing?"

"Give me a hand — we haven't got much time," Miles snapped. "Did you hear what this bird said about a phony American general being parachuted into Brey?"

"I heard," Lute said grimly. "I was playin' possum about then, waiting to see what happened."

"We're going to try it in reverse," Miles said, busily unbuttoning Holtz's tunic. "I've got a hunch that this uniform is going to get us out of the German lines and back to Brey."

"I've heard a lot of screwy ideas," Lute said

grudgingly. "This one might work. What about me?"

"We'll pick you up a German helmet and over-coat once we get out of here," Miles said. "Help me with his breeches."

It was two o'clock in the morning as Miles settled the dead German's peaked cap on his head and took a last look around the room. They'd crammed Holtz's body into a chest in one corner and there was nothing here to show that everything wasn't as it should be, he decided. Lute squinted critically.

"You make a good lookin' *obersturmbannführer*," he said. "You give any thought to what the first G.I. we run into is going to do when he sees us duded up like a couple of vons, Miles?"

"We'll worry about that when we come to it," Boone said. "Put out the light and go out ahead of me. If anyone challenges us, I'm taking you for questioning."

They went along a short hallway, Lute ahead, and stepped boldly out into the night. A sentry beside the door challenged and Miles answered harshly. The sentry answered respectfully, drawing himself up and clicking his heels as Boone and Heard turned the corner. Rigny still burned but the eerie light was in their favor — enough to see by but not enough to give them away. The house they had been in was on a side street just off the square and Miles turned back in that direction.

They paused in the shadows by the corner and their luck was in. The jeep was standing where they'd left it just across the way with a German soldier guarding it.

"There's your helmet and overcoat," Miles said softly. Other Germans moved about the square. "I'll send him over here where it's dark. Can you handle him?"

"Give me that gun. I'll handle him!"

The soldier by the jeep went docilely toward the side street at Boone's order. He returned a few minutes later but he had lost stature in the process. His long overcoat now flapped below his ankles as he slid behind the wheel of the jeep. No one in the square paid any attention as the engine caught and the vehicle moved toward the Brey road.

"Have any trouble?" Miles asked in a low voice as they left the square behind.

Lute chuckled evilly. "Nope. I didn't need the gun. Used a paving block. I wish I had hit him harder — this coat stinks."

The Germans were wasting no time, Miles saw as the jeep wove in and out of traffic on the Brey road. They passed a column of supply vehicles and then what he took to be a battalion of motorized artillery. The tail of an armored column showed dimly ahead and they passed tanks, infantry riding on their hulls and the heads and shoulders of the tank commanders showing above open hatches. Now and then a voice called out angrily as Lute cut in too sharply. It was three-quarters of an hour later when the road ahead showed its length empty in the starlight.

"You think that's the last of 'em?" Lute asked.

"It could be," Miles answered.

"Then why don't we get rid of these clothes before some trigger-happy G.I. shoots our heads off?"

"Not yet," Miles said. He'd been thinking of the road net he had studied so carefully at Couteaux. "They may still come in handy."

Again he went over the map in his mind. This road ran generally southwest to reach the Vaar at Brey, he knew. It didn't run straight; it meandered in lazy turns to avoid the low marshes as it neared the Vaar. A faint excitement stirred Miles as he remembered that at one of those turns, where the road ran almost northwest for a short stretch, a road from Vaaracre came in. If he could direct the following German column into that road. . . .

Once the lead vehicles had entered, the others would follow. He thought back to Saint Heye and remembered young Dunn's scout car there directing traffic away from Bastogne. There was just a chance that he could do the same, shunting the Brey column towards Vaaracre. There it would jam head-on into the German column which undoubtedly was already moving on the main Rigny-Vaaracre road. With the bridge at Vaaracre out, the German drive could be stalled for another twenty-four hours. It was worth a try.

"Step on it," he said to Lute.

"I already am," Lute said. "I don't yearn none to see no more Germans tonight."

"You probably will," Miles said.

They rode for another half hour, the road curving first in one direction and then another. They went through shallow patches of woods which further confused the sense of direction. The possibility that his scheme might succeed grew on Boone as they went. The point where the Vaaracre road came in should be close now.

They came to it ten minutes later and Boone breathed a little prayer. The god of battles must be on his side tonight, he thought, because even the terrain lent itself to his plan. The road had been running through one of the intermittent patches of woods, and it forked as it emerged here. The right-hand fork ran straight ahead; the left-hand fork turned deeper into the woods which stretched away southward. He saw a signpost in the dim light as he dropped a hand on Lute's arm.

"Stop here!" he said.

Lute stepped on the brake and Miles was down into the snow before the vehicle stopped rolling. With the aid of the dead SS officer's lighter, Boone read the signs. They were nailed one above the other making a V on the post. One said: VAARACRE — 20 KILOMETRES. The other: BREY — 15 KILOMETRES.

"Give me a hand," Miles snapped. "Bring a tire iron! Anything to hammer with!"

They knocked the Brey sign loose; then hammered it back at an angle to point up the Vaaracre road. The Vaaracre sign they threw into the brush. "You don't think they'll be stupid enough to believe this?" Lute asked. "Somebody'll have a map."

"We won't give him time to use it," Miles said. "You and I are going to be right here directing traffic."

"What!"

"You heard me," Miles said tightly.

"Now I know I should have skipped this war," Lute said mournfully.

"It's got a chance," Miles said. "The drivers are dead beat after Rigny — they're not going to argue. No officer under the grade of a full colonel is going to give an *obersturmbannführer* any back talk, either. The Germans know their SS characters."

"I hope you're right," Lute said.

It was a half hour later when they heard the low grumble of diesel engines in the starlight; ten minutes after that the slit headlights of the first tanks showed through the trees. The lead tank came on. Miles, standing in the middle of the fork that led to Brey, waved the vehicle on down the Vaaracre road. The second followed and then the next. Most of a company had gone by when a Volkswagen skidded to a stop at the crossroads. A voice called out angrily — immediately dropped to a tone of respect as passing tank lights showed Boone's SS uniform.

"Are we on the right road for Brey, sir?" it asked.

"You are," Miles snapped in German. "Proceed!"

"At once, sir! Heil Hitler!"

"Heil Hitler!" Miles said.

Boone guessed that a good half of the tank column had gone by, when Lute touched his arm. They had done all they could do here; it was time they were getting on.

Lute said, "We better haul out of here, Miles. I got a feeling that this thing is just about to bust wide open."

"Get the jeep started," Miles said.

He heard the engine kick over behind him, was about to turn when he saw a car, its headlights on, coming toward him quickly as it paralleled the tank column. Here was trouble — maybe bad trouble — he knew as he loosened Holtz's pistol in the holster at his hip. It was a German staff car and it came to a halt a few yards away. A voice shouted angrily.

"What goes on here? Who are you?"

Boone answered in German, hoping that his accent wasn't too noticeable and that his voice sounded as an SS officer's would. "Lieutenant Colonel Holtz, sir." From the tone of the voice of the man who had challenged him he knew that he was dealing with no junior officer. "On a special mission."

"Come here and identify yourself properly, Colonel!"

Boone moved back toward the closed car. In the dim light he saw that only two men were in it, the driver and a passenger in the back. He laid hold

of the door handle with his left hand and opened
it, standing close so that his right hand was hidden
as it dropped to the Luger at his hip.

"Gladly, sir," he said. "May I ask to whom I am
speaking?" The voice that answered him was cold
and suspicious.

"General Menkeil of the Fifth SS Panzer Brigade," it said. "Your identification, Colonel!"

"Here it is," Boone said as he opened the door
wider and pointed the gun at the man who sat
there. "Tell your driver not to move or I will
shoot, General!"

For a split second there was silence while Miles
wondered if he had gambled and lost. Then General Menkeil spat words at the chauffeur and the
latter froze. "I'll strangle you with my own hands
for this," the German general added as Boone
climbed in beside him and slammed the door.

"We'll talk about strangling later," Miles said
coldly. "Now tell your driver to turn down the left-
hand road."

Boone prayed that Lute had been watching and
had guessed what had happened. He breathed a
sigh of relief as he saw the jeep start to move down
the Brey road ahead of them. Keeping the Luger
jammed against Menkeil's side, he took the other's
side arm from him and thrust it into his own empty
holster.

"Keep your head to the front and drive carefully," he said to the driver. "You'll get a bullet
through your neck, if you don't. General, permit me

to properly introduce myself now. I am Miles Boone, brigadier general, United States Army. You are my prisoner."

Major General Clark Blocker had his command post in what had once been the mayor's office in Brey. It was nine o'clock in the morning and Colonel Watson, his chief of staff, had just been in to tell him that the first elements of Combat Command B were beginning to enter the bridgehead which the Hammerhead Division held here at Brey.

"Boone with them?" Blocker had asked.

"I didn't learn, sir," Watson had said. "I presume that he must be but I'll find out."

"I want to see him," Blocker had said.

Now Blocker sat in his chair and looked out of the window at the gray sky and thought. He was going to have to eat crow, he guessed, when Miles Boone arrived. There could be no doubt about it — the defense that Boone had put up at Rigny had been epic.

Corps had estimated that parts, at least, of five German divisions had hit Rigny from three sides. That a single combat command should hold the place for even one day would have been almost a miracle. That Combat Command B had held it for four days was a miracle four times over. He should know. The rest of the Hammerhead Division had been battered badly enough holding the bridgehead here at Brey.

Colonel Watson's tap came at the door again and

the chief of staff stepped inside. He wore an odd expression on his face, Blocker thought. He dismissed it as his thoughts returned to Miles Boone and Combat Command B.

"Well?" he asked.

"Colonel Nash is here, sir," Watson said.

"Nash! What's he doing here? Where is Boone, Watson? He's the one I want to see!"

"Sir," Colonel Watson said cautiously, "I understand that General Boone didn't return from Rigny with Combat Command B. Colonel Nash brought it in."

"Who told you that?"

"Colonel Nash, sir."

Eight

COLONEL NELSON NASH, feet thrust out in front of him, slouched in a chair in the office of the chief of staff of the Hammerhead Armored Division while he waited for General Blocker to call for him. A four days' growth of dirty beard decorated Nash's even, patrician features. Grimy tape covered a gash on his forehead. His trousers were muddy and torn at one knee and there were bloodstains on his field jacket.

He was aware of how he looked and it gave him a sharp satisfaction. He wore the appearance of a man who had been in a mean, desperate battle for the last four days — a man who had acquitted himself very well — and all of that was true, he was telling himself now. Furthermore, it had been he who had led Combat Command B on its night march from Rigny and had brought it safely into the bridgehead here at Brey this morning.

It was no fault of his that Miles Boone was missing. Boone should have stayed with his Command; he had no business remaining back there in Rigny doing a major's job. Nash was pretty sure that was the way that General Blocker would see it. Back in Couteaux — that seemed a long while ago now — he had decided to play it easy and let Boone hang himself. Now it looked as though Boone had done just that.

He'd say no more to Blocker than he had to, Nash decided. Things left unsaid could be just as damaging and, anyway, the facts spoke for themselves. Boone had been alive when Combat Command B had pulled out of Rigny; Boone was not with Combat Command B now. Those were the facts. Nash had no intentions of weakening them by trying to interpret them for General Blocker.

The inner door opened and Colonel Watson, the chief of staff, nodded at Nash. "Come in, Colonel."

He let Nash pass and then closed the door. Nash saluted. Blocker sat in his customary pose, big fists clenched on the desk, while he looked at Nash from beneath heavy brows.

"You look like you'd been in a fight," he said.

"We have, sir," Nash answered, exaggerating his tiredness a little as he sat down. "It was pretty rough at times, General, but we hung onto Rigny until dark last night."

"I know that," Blocker said drily. His next question was the one Nash had been waiting for. "Where's Boone?"

"I don't know, sir." Nash chose his words carefully now. "He remained in Rigny last night when Combat Command B moved out. I haven't seen or heard from him since."

"He put you in acting command of CCB?"

"Yes, sir, until he rejoined." Nash tried to keep the smugness out of his voice. "He hasn't rejoined."

"What orders did he give you?"

"Orders, sir? Why, to retire toward Brey, sir."

Blocker's voice turned flinty. "Did he tell you that during the withdrawal Combat Command B would continue to block the Rigny road and cover the north flank of the rest of the division as it retires west of the Vaar today?"

"Uh . . . yes, sir," Nash said, floundering a little as his mind sought a way out of this. "I believe that General Boone did say something about that. He wasn't very specific, sir . . ."

"Specific!" Blocker spat the word. "What's there to be specific about, Colonel? Your mission is to keep the Germans from hitting the flank of the rest of the division while it's spread out across the Vaar! Isn't that plain enough for you? Where's Combat Command B now?"

"In Brey, sir," Nash said. "We're low on gas and ammunition and the men are pretty well used up. I thought a few hours' rest . . ."

"Rest!" Blocker's words hit like sledges. "This whole division's been put through a meat grinder since Saturday. Everybody needs a rest. They won't get it! The whole Ardennes front has caved in. The Germans could reach the Meuse and the war be lost in the next few days. And you talk of rest!"

"Sir, I didn't . . ."

Blocker cut him off. "All right, then, *I'll* be

specific! You take CCB back to that roadblock outside Brey. Until you get direct orders from here to withdraw, you hold the Rigny road as long as you've got a tank that can move or a man that can pull a trigger! Is that clear?"

"Yes, sir," Nash said hollowly.

Nash went back through the outer office, his face white and his eyes bitter. He'd take his time about getting back to the roadblock, he decided resentfully. At least he'd get gas and ammunition.

The chief of staff went back into General Blocker's office as soon as Nash had left. The dark, brooding look on the general's face warned Colonel Watson that there was trouble ahead. He thought that he knew what kind of trouble.

"Did you learn anything of the whereabouts of General Boone, sir?" he asked cautiously.

"I learned all I need to learn," Blocker said. "Boone stayed behind with the covering screen. The chances are that by now he's either captured or dead. What has happened to him is not important — what *is* important is that he is not here now at a time when I need him most!"

"Are you leaving Nash in command of CCB?"

"What choice have I got?" Blocker rasped. "I was beginning to think I had something good in Boone. Now I've got nothing."

The chief of staff shook his head soberly. "Boone did the thing he thought best, sir," he said. "At least it took guts to stay up there with the screen . . ."

"Guts!" Blocker said but his voice was milder now. "We've got millions of men with guts. We haven't got millions of commanders. War is directed force. The force best directed will win. It is my job to direct a small part of that force and I do it through my own commanders. When one of them allows himself to be killed or captured he has deprived me of a part of my means to exert force."

"Death is unavoidable sometimes, sir. You relied a lot on Benny Martell — yet he . . ."

"I know that it's unavoidable, confound it!" Blocker snapped, his temper returning. "There's this difference — Benny got it because his time had run out. He didn't get it because he was running around looking for it — trying to plug every leaky dike with his own finger. That's what Boone's been doing and that's the reason I've got to depend now on someone like Nash!"

A dour gray dawn was seeping through the firs as the road wound toward the edge of the woods that showed a couple of hundred yards ahead. General Menkeil and his driver, trussed back to back, rode in the rear of the jeep. Earlier the general of the Fifth SS Panzer Brigade had protested violently against the indignity of being tied up — and to a common soldier, at that. Miles Boone had shut him up. He'd taken about all that he intended to take from the SS for one night.

"We ought to be runnin' into some of our boys

pretty soon," Lute Heard said. "You ought to get shet of them German duds, Miles, now that it's getting light."

"And wear what — my underwear?" Boone asked crossly. "I'm half frozen as it is."

"Yeah, I didn't think of that," Lute said.

He had gotten rid of his own German helmet and overcoat when they'd stopped to tie up the general and his driver. It had been no chore for Lute — the borrowed garments had been worn over his own. Boone's breeches and field jacket had been left behind in Rigny. They drove on in silence, jolting over the bad road, and had almost reached the edge of the woods when a rifle shot rang out in the cold air and a bullet slammed into the jeep's side. A man showed in the road ahead, rifle held ready. More men came from the bushes beside the road.

"Halt and get your hands up!" a rough voice said. It had a Brooklyn accent and sounded mean. "Fast!"

Lute tramped on the brake, bringing the jeep to a sudden stop in the road as more G.I.s boiled out of the brush. Boone knew none of the faces but he had little doubt as to what their grim expressions meant — it was spelled out plainly in hostile eyes. These Americans, fighting for their lives now, were in no mood to deal gently with Germans caught within their lines, riding stolen jeeps and one wearing an American uniform.

A big infantryman, carrying a tommy gun,

reached for Lute and yanked him down into the snow. "Hold it!" Boone ordered. "We're Americans. I'm ..."

He did not get a chance to finish the sentence before rough hands laid hold of him and dumped him on his face in the road. A heavy boot slammed against his ribs, driving the breath out of him so that he gagged and was almost sick. From what seemed a great distance, he heard a voice calling with authority.

"All right! All right!" it was saying. "Take it easy, men. Let's see what we've got here!"

"A pair of Germans, Lootenant," another voice answered angrily. "One of 'em wearin' G.I.s! I say we don't mess none with 'em! We deal with 'em right here!"

"Wait a minute, Sergeant. There's something funny about this. Who are those two tied up in back?"

The rough voice became more impatient as Boone shook his head to clear it and got to his knees. "I didn't ask 'em, Lootenant. Germans, too, I reckon. We can handle four as easy as two. All right, you guys, hustle them out here!"

Lute's voice came from the far side of the jeep. "You knuckle-headed baboon!" it said hoarsely. "Lay a hand on me again and I'll bust you wide open! I was soldiering in this man's Army before you'd learned to wipe your nose! Those two are our prisoners and ..."

"You asked for it," the sergeant's voice said, as

Boone reached a hand to the jeep and pulled himself up.

"Lieutenant," Boone said, trying to put authority into his voice and finding it difficult because not all of his breath had come back yet, "I am General Miles Boone, commanding CCB of the Hammerhead Armored Division. That man is Sergeant Heard, my driver and orderly. The two in back are German prisoners. Take me to your commanding officer at once!"

"Yes, sir," the lieutenant said. "I suppose you have some identification, General? There's been a lot of Germans infiltrating our lines and we can't take chances."

"I've got no identification," Boone snapped. "It was taken from me when I was a German prisoner in Rigny. We're wasting time! I want to see your C.O. at once!"

Lieutenant Poole said crisply, "Form an escort for the prisoners. We're taking them back."

Major Abe Abernathy had his command post in a farmhouse that stood a little back from the Rigny road. He was a chubby, red-cheeked man, fussy in his habits but solid in a fight. He sat at a table while Miles Boone stood in front of him, a soldier with a tommy gun guarding the closed door of the room.

"The way you tell it, it sounds okay . . . General," Abernathy said, half convinced. "The trouble is, all these other birds we've caught had good stories, too. You know anybody around here who could identify you?"

"Anyone in Combat Command B can identify me," Boone said impatiently. "General Blocker can identify me."

"Yeah, I guess that's right. Trouble is, Combat Command B is back in Brey by now," Abernathy said. "They passed through here before daylight."

Miles scowled; Nash should have taken over the roadblock right here. "What do you mean — passed through?" he demanded. "They didn't stop?"

Abernathy shook his head. "A colonel named Nash talked with me a couple of minutes. He didn't say anything about stopping. I guess the best thing for me to do is send you under guard to Brey, too, General . . ."

"How about the reserve? Has it passed through?"

"Haven't seen it. Now, if . . ."

Abernathy was interrupted by a captain who thrust his head into the room. "Hey, Abe," he said warningly, "some captain by the name of Ziegler just showed up and is looking for General Boone. Maybe he can identify these men for us."

"Bud Ziegler!" Miles said, turning.

It was Ziegler in his leather coat with the ripped sleeve and a dirty bandage around his head. Behind him was a score of men. Miles had seen them before, retiring stubbornly through the narrow streets of the burning Rigny, fighting a vicious, dogged battle as they went.

"What the outright perdition is this, General,

seh?" Bud asked, stalking forward. "Kind of looks like these heah silly monkeys was fixin' it to shoot you. They plumb crazy?"

Miles explained in a few words.

"This heah's General Boone," Ziegler concluded. "He mighty near defended Rigny all by his lone self. Then he comes back heah and you rear area apes want to shoot him!"

Miles Boone was sitting behind the table in Abernathy's command post with a steaming canteen cup of coffee at his elbow. Bud Ziegler, chewing on a K-ration candy bar, lounged in one corner, the sleepy expression back in his eyes.

"Real glad to find you heah, seh," Ziegler said. "We was right upsot when we had to skedaddle out of Rigny without you. Figured, though, you'd take care of yoahse'f."

"Lucky for me you showed up when you did," Boone grunted. "What happened — did you have to come across country?"

Ziegler nodded. "We all kept to the road foah about a mile out of town," he said. Then he frowned thoughtfully. "Afteh a little, German tanks come a-whoopin' behind us so we took to the hills. Something funny heah, General. It jest come to me that them tanks ought to be knockin' at ouah door right now."

"We delayed them a little," Boone said.

He spoke briefly of how the German column had been diverted along the Vaaracre road. A look of pleased appreciation spread over the major's long features as he unfolded himself from the table, slapping his leg softly.

"Doggone," he said in his lazy drawl. "I don' reckon that General Lee could of done it no betteh, seh."

"By now they've discovered their mistake," Boone said soberly. "They'll be pushing down this road before long. Abernathy says that the division is withdrawing across the Vaar today. This place has got to be held until the withdrawal is complete or the Germans will smash the division's flank, then everything goes up in smoke. Abernathy hasn't enough of a force here to meet the kind of attack that is coming."

"Combat Command B ain't heah, seh?"

Boone shook his head. "Nash took it on towards Brey," he said. "I want you to go after it and bring it back, Bud. Take Heard and the jeep. Issue orders in my name — do anything you have to do — but bring Combat Command B back!"

"I'll shore do that, seh."

After Ziegler had gone, Miles sat at the table for a moment longer, trying to sort out his thoughts with a brain which was fuzzy from lack of sleep. When Combat Command B had withdrawn from Rigny it had still the mission of protecting the Rigny road from German advance from the northeast. That should have been plain to Nash. Well, the damage was done. All that he could do now was to hang on with what Abernathy had here and hope that the Germans didn't hit before Ziegler got back with CCB.

That last hope was dissipated as Abernathy came back in, his chubby face agitated. "One of my patrols has just reported a strong German armored column four miles northeast of here advancing down the Rigny road, sir," he said. "The patrol leader estimates its strength at a panzer brigade!"

Boone stood up. "Very well," he heard himself saying. "We'd better get ready to meet it."

Major Abernathy was staring at him, shocked. "General," he said, his voice disbelieving, "I've only got two companies of armored infantry here plus a couple of tank destroyers! We can't stop a panzer brigade!"

"We can try," Boone said.

As he went out into the cold morning he was trying to remember each detail of the road he had come along earlier. He had a feeling that there was something important about the road, but it eluded his tired mind. Just a road, not too wide, running almost straight through, perhaps, four hundred yards of woods. Dense, dark woods where the firs stood close together like ranked sentries. Where had he heard of another such road?

Then he had it. Braddock! The British general who had been trapped on a narrow track where his heavy column could not maneuver or deploy against an enemy, hidden by the trees, who struck at him from all sides. In the woods the Nazi column would be in the same situation, unable to get off the road because of the trees and unable to bring its overwhelmingly superior fire power to bear. It might work — it was worth a try!

New life surged through Boone as he caught Abernathy by the shoulder. "Have you got any antitank mines?"

"Sir?"

Miles explained his plan swiftly. They'd mine the road where it debouched from the woods — knock out the first tanks and block the way for the rest. The two tank destroyers, firing down the road, could get any tanks that came through. The two infantry companies, deployed in the heavy growth on either side of the road, would attack the German column with bazookas and grenades. Maybe they'd not hurt the Germans too much but the confusion would hold them in place until Combat Command B arrived.

"By gosh, it might work!" Abernathy said, a little awe in his face as he looked at Boone. "I've got an engineer detachment with me. It ought to have some mines."

He left on the run. The cold air was beginning to clear Boone's head now as he looked at the edge of the woods a quarter mile away. They hadn't much time and they'd have to move fast. A radio man came through the door behind him.

"General," the radio man said hastily, "there's a Colonel Nash wants to talk to you."

Boone was about to answer that he had no time

to talk with Nash now — thought better of it and turned back towards the house. "Where's the radio?" he asked.

"Here, sir."

Nash's voice came to him, distorted by static. Combat Command B was still in Brey, it said. It was gassing up — couldn't move for another half hour. Meanwhile, that crazy infantryman, Ziegler, was trying to throw his weight around.

Boone spoke into the mike. Nash would get CCB back here to Abernathy's blocking position if he had to carry the tanks on his back. When he got here he would take on the Nazi armored brigade that he, Boone, would be fighting with rifles in the woods! Did Nash understand?

"Yes, sir," Nash said. "Out."

Another voice said, "You, Boone, hold on! I've been having every channel monitored in the hope I'd get you. What is this about a Nazi panzer brigade?"

It was General Blocker. Boone told him the situation in curt words. When he had finished there was silence for a moment. Then Blocker's voice came again and there was a subtle change in its quality. Boone was too tired to care.

"You think that you can hold, Boone, until I can get Combat Command B there?"

"I'll hold," he said.

"That's all I wanted to know," Blocker said. "Out."

Well, that was that, Miles was thinking without caring much about it as he went back into the gray morning. It was starting to snow again, he saw; feathery stuff that drifted lazily down. That was all to the good. It would decrease visibility and provide additional concealment. Abernathy was waiting for him, new purpose showing in his chubby face. He had the commanders of his two armored infantry companies with him, together with the tank destroyer lieutenant and the sergeant of engineers.

Boone's plan was full blown in his mind now and he gave it to them quickly — saw the skepticism which had first marked their faces turn first to a grudging acceptance and finally to a faint enthusiasm. "Questions?" he asked.

"This is the first time I ever heard of fighting Tiger tanks with rifles," one of the infantry captains said. "Just because I never heard of it don't say it can't be done."

Boone gave him an approving look. "If the sergeant gets his mines laid right," he said, "there'll be a spectacular amount of confusion at first. Tank commanders will unbutton their hatches to get a look at what's going on. That'll give our riflemen a chance to pick them off or pop a grenade into the hatch. That makes for more confusion. Get the picture?"

They nodded. The engineer sergeant, a frecklefaced kid, spat and grinned. "Them mines will be laid all right, General," he said with superb selfconfidence. "Don't you worry none."

"Then let's go," Boone said.

Two columns of infantrymen were already moving toward the woods along the road. Miles lingered behind for a moment, discussing with the tank destroyer lieutenant where the latter would put his self-propelled guns. The boy had good ideas. One on either side to scissor the gap where the German tanks had to leave the woods, if they left at all. That would bring them under flanking fire at the point where they were most vulnerable.

"Right," Boone said. "Good luck, son."

It was not quite nine o'clock and snowing heavily as Boone clumped through the trees toward the center of the line where Able Company of the armored infantry lay hidden in its ambush. He had done all that he could do, he knew. The mines were planted, the tank destroyers in position. The infantry, bazookas strategically placed, made a thin line that ran a half mile along either side of the road. Abernathy was on the far side. There was nothing to do now but wait.

Boone sat down in the snow with his back against a tree; picked up a handful of the cold, white stuff and rubbed it over his face. Suddenly he was thinking of that day in Dobbs Ferry again. The snow there had been just as white and just as soft. He would like to go back to Dobbs Ferry someday, taking Janet with him. Impatiently he shook the thought away.

A new sound had come into the morning — a sound that he had gotten to know well in the last few days. It was the grumble of diesel engines and the metallic clank of tank treads.

The column seemed endless to Boone as he lay behind his screen of brush and watched the big tanks clank by scarcely a dozen yards away. There was an awesome sense of power in the way they moved. Miles had started to count when the lead tank had passed — now he had reached one hundred and still that first mine had not gone off.

"One hundred three . . . one hundred four . . ."

Had something gone wrong with the mines, he wondered, a cold hand gripping the pit of his stomach. Everything depended on the head of the column being blocked before it got out of the woods — the rest of the column being forced to recoil on itself. If that didn't happen the road would be open to Brey and the Hammerhead Division would be dead.

Then a dull boom broke the morning apart. It was followed by another. Then two more. In front of Boone the column began a slow halt, rear tanks crowding those in front. Somewhere a man yelled angrily. Hatches were opening as tank commanders thrust heads and shoulders out to see what was wrong ahead.

"Now!" Boone said under his breath.

It was as though he had pulled the string of an invisible detonator which set the dark firs shuddering beneath a bedlam of sound. Machine guns hidden beside the road started their crazy laughter; M-1s, with their heavier bark, and tommy guns

joined in. The hoarse *bar . . . ung* of exploding
grenades punctuated the rataplan. Over it all lifted
another sound that raised goose pimples along
Boone's spine.

It was the sound of men's voices eddying up-
ward in a wordless shout. The chant of men who
lived now only to kill. It was awesome, barbaric.

So had men chanted at the Alamo, and on Ceme-
tery Ridge at Gettysburg, at San Juan Hill and
in the Argonne. Miles Boone found that he was
yelling with the rest.

The German in the turret of the tank opposite
Boone was slumped, half in and half out of the
hatch. A doughboy scrambled up on the hull and
tossed a grenade into the half-open hatch. There
was a muffled roar and the tank belched smoke,
then began to burn. The doughboy turned to jump
down. He stopped, a foot half-lifted and a surprised look on his face, as a burst of machine-gun
fire caught him. He fell between two tanks.

Boone ran toward him and was dragging him
back to the shelter of the bushes when the scythe
of the machine-gun fire reached for them. It spun
Boone around and flung him on his face in the
snow. He tried to get to his hands and knees but
it took too much effort and he slid forward again,
vaguely grateful for the coolness of the snow
against his cheek. His mind had become curiously
clear of all thought.

Tanks were fighting back now, their turret guns
booming — futile fire that seared the firs but could

not be depressed enough to reach the men lying below. Here and there a Tiger had spun around in the road so that its bow guns could be fired. The advantage of the attackers couldn't last, Boone knew vaguely, but there was nothing that he could do about it now. The vague thought died as he heard a new sound now, faint but unmistakable. The gruff bark of the guns of Sherman tanks. Combat Command B was coming up!

Consciousness came slowly back to Boone. He lay still, looking up at the ceiling of a room and wondering, without caring very much, where he was. After a moment the pain began enveloping his left side. Bits of the fight began to come back to him now. Then he remembered that he had heard Combat Command B coming up and he felt better. A good outfit — CCB.

A voice said gruffly, "It's about time you come out of it! Since when does two or three slugs get a good cavalryman down?" It was Lute Heard's voice.

Miles turned his head painfully. Lute was sitting beside him in a chair and there was no mistaking the relief in the older man's red, hatchet-sharp face.

"Hello, Lute," Miles said. "So you and Nash finally brought up CCB, did you?"

"Nash and me and General Blocker," Lute said, his voice still gruff. "The old rowdy was leadin' the parade in the first tank. Nash was a holy terror, the way he fought. I think he could have licked them Germans by hisself. Even Blocker was pleased, and told him so."

Miles was silent for a moment. He suddenly felt relieved and immensely pleased to hear this, especially from Lute Heard. It was the highest praise.

Nash had made his mistakes, but there had been nothing wrong with the way he had fought at Rigny. And now he had fully justified Boone's faith in him.

"Well, I better get your stuff together," Lute said. "They're shipping you to a hospital."

"How bad . . . ?" Miles began.

"Not bad enough you won't be out raisin' Cain in about a month," Lute said sourly. "Provided that red-headed dame from Couteaux don't bribe the docs to keep you in. Which I don't bet she won't. It might be a good thing, at that, you've gone nutty enough to fight tanks with your bare hands."

All at once Miles felt much better. "We'll see," he said.

In another room Colonel Watson eyed General Blocker sardonically. "So you were riding a tank," he said. "Funny. I seem to remember a lecture you gave me earlier this morning about another general doing just that. Something about fingers in dikes, wasn't it, sir?"

Blocker looked a little abashed — an alien expression for him. "So I ought to be kicked," he growled. "So maybe I was wrong and Boone was right. So maybe I'll hang a medal on the guy just to let him know it."

"The best idea you've had today," Watson said.